To Gemma

Merry Christmas

all my love

from

Granny + Grandad

THE PRISM TREE

By the same author
Beyond the Rolling River

THE PRISM TREE

Kate Andrew

Illustrated by Chris Riddell

COLLINS

To Mam

William Collins Sons & Co Ltd
London · Glasgow · Sydney · Auckland
Toronto · Johannesburg

First published 1990
© text Kate Andrew 1990
© illustrations Chris Riddell 1990

A CIP catalogue record for this book
is available from the British Library.

ISBN 0 00 184743-0

Printed and Bound in Great Britain by
Hartnolls Limited, Bodmin, Cornwall.

Contents

Chapter 1 ~ Pirates Bold

"I love to be a Pirate King
And sail the seven seas,
I love to watch my prisoners
Go down upon their knees,
And when they beg for mercy
And they want to call it quits,
I chip 'em and I chop 'em
Into very little bits!

I tell them interesting tales
Of drownings and of bones,
With jolly little choruses
All filled with gruesome groans,
And when they are so terrified
They've nearly lost their wits,
I chip 'em and I chop 'em
Into very little bits!

I'm really quite impartial,
As a Pirate King should be –
A captain or a cabin boy
Is all the same to me,
And whether they are Russians
Or Americans or Brits,
I chip 'em and I chop 'em
Into very little bits!"

The captain of the clipper finished his song by swishing his cutlass through the air. The skinny pilot standing next to him holding the steering wheel jumped with fright.

"What's the matter, Weedy?" asked the captain with a grin. "Afraid I was going to cut your tail off, or something?"

The pilot said nothing, but looked back at his tail. It was long and handsome, and covered in silvery scales. The captain's tail was also scaly, like the rest of his body, but in his case the scales were of an in-between colour that shone sometimes blue, sometimes green, according to the light. In fact, he was more or less the colour of the sea, which he considered very appropriate for a bold sea-captain.

Apart from the scales, and the fact that they had webbed feet, the captain and the pilot, along with the rest of the crew, looked like very large cats.

They were, in fact, nethercats, born and bred under water, though they could live very well on dry land. And while they might disagree about other things, they were all agreed that nethercats were the handsomest, bravest and cleverest animals in the world.

On top of that, the captain was feeling particularly pleased with himself just now. He had a brand new sailing ship, a hand-picked (well, paw-picked) crew, plenty of stores and a favourable wind. It was true they had not exactly captured anything yet, but that was only a matter of time. And besides the pirating venture, he had another little scheme tucked away at the back of his mind.

Somewhere on their travels they were sure to meet a certain type of small animal with unusual powers. Once he had captured one and learned its secret, nothing could stop him from ruling the land as well as the sea.

"After all, you can't make an omelette if you keep all your eggs in one basket," he murmured to himself. "Look after the roundabouts, and the swings will take care of themselves." One way or the other, he was sure Captain Slubblejum was going to come out on top.

Chapter 2 ~ All at Sea

Toby Jones was spending the spring half-term in the Lake District with his grandma, who was an Artist of Distinction. She had started teaching him to paint with real oil paints, but the second day he was beginning to get bored with that. After lunch, Grandma showed him where to find a small rowing boat in the shed near the lake.

"You can have a nice row on the lake while I am painting," she said. "Just look at those trees with the light on them! Don't go too far, will you, dear?"

"Don't worry," said Toby, as he settled himself in the boat. "I won't stay out long." He checked his new waterproof alarm watch, and couldn't resist making it chime *Jingle Bells* just once more.

"That tune is driving me crazy!" said his grandma. Toby pushed the boat off hurriedly.

It was a fine, warm afternoon, and after a few

minutes he shipped the oars and just let the boat drift along in the spring sunshine. He adjusted the watch strap, which tended to slip, and then sat back and relaxed. *This is the life!* he thought, as he closed his eyes, and felt the warm sun on his face.

He only opened them again when he realized it had grown much cooler. A breeze had sprung up, making little waves on the lake. Quite big waves, in fact. As he started rowing again, he dipped the oars in the water at the wrong moment, pulled hard on empty air, and fell flat on his back. As he picked himself up, he saw that one of the oars had gone, and was bobbing away merrily on the crest of a big wave.

Surely the waves shouldn't be *that* big? A nasty little suspicion formed in his mind, and he leaned over the side of the boat and got some of the water in his cupped hands. He sipped at it cautiously, then spat it out. It was salty, and very bitter. There was no doubt about it, he had somehow drifted out to the open sea.

His first reaction was to be very indignant. He ran his fingers through his sandy hair, making it stick out like bits of straw, and sat muttering to himself. *Why didn't someone tell me there was a channel leading out to the sea? There should be a notice, or a buoy or something.* Then he realized that he had no food, no drinking water, and only

one oar, and he began to get rather frightened.

Well, it was no use just sitting there feeling frightened. He started trying to use the one oar as a paddle, but it was not easy to do, and soon he was feeling very seasick and miserable. Then, suddenly, he caught a glimpse of something that made him open his blue eyes very wide. It disappeared as the rowing boat slid down the side of the next wave, but a moment later, there it was again – an old-fashioned sailing ship, with three great masts, and the wind filling its strong, white sails.

Toby felt extremely relieved that rescue was at hand, but the ship was bearing down on him too fast for comfort. Its strange, carved figurehead seemed to threaten him as it rushed towards him – it was a cat-like creature with a fierce expression, clutching in its outstretched hand the sort of whip he recognized as a cat-o'-nine tails. However, he didn't have time to wonder about it because he was too busy trying to kneel up in the bobbing rowing boat, and wave his arms in the air.

"Help! Help!" he shouted. "Don't run me down! Help! Rescue!"

His cries must have been heard, because someone on the deck threw a rope ladder over the ship's side just as the rowing boat was about to bump into it. Toby took a flying leap, grabbed

the rope ladder, and scrambled up it as fast as he could go. The rowing boat spun round wildly as he jumped, then drifted off in the wake of the ship and was lost to sight.

Toby climbed up to the deck rail, noticing the name painted on the ship's side – *Catty Sark*. He felt someone pulling him over onto the deck, straightened up to thank his rescuer, and found himself looking into the cat-like, whiskery face of his old enemy, Slubblejum.

A few months ago, Toby had foiled a plan of Slubblejum's to make himself King of the World, and he thought he had seen the last of him for ever. Now his mouth fell open, and he just gaped at the nethercat in astonishment. Slubblejum's mouth remained firmly closed, mainly because he was holding something between his teeth. When Toby got his voice back, all he could think of to say was, "What on earth have you got in your mouth?"

"Yit ya yutyass," said Slubblejum.

"What?" said Toby. "Oh, a *cutlass*. Well, why are you carrying it between your teeth?"

"Yat yot yirate hoo," said Slubblejum. Then he decided to take the cutlass out of his mouth, and repeated, "That's what pirates do. When they take prisoners, you know."

"Did you say *pirates*?" asked Toby. "And *prisoners*?" He looked round and noticed that more nethercats were approaching from all sides to see what was going on. There were about a dozen of them, in various colours and sizes, their cats' eyes full of curiosity as they stood around and stared at him.

"What are you doing here anyway?" went on Slubblejum, ignoring Toby's question. "Spying on us, are you?"

"Not at all!" said Toby. "I just went rowing on a lake and found myself out at sea."

"Look before you leap if you want to keep your head above water," pronounced Slubblejum. Then a sly little grin spread over his face. "But you may just be a lucky break for us. Have you got that thing with you?"

"What thing?" asked Toby in surprise.

"You know, that changing-colour thing – the chamelyeron."

Toby remembered the chameleon with the odd name, Hardly Visible, who had gone with him on his last adventure, and there was something about Slubblejum's face that made him feel glad his small friend was safe at home.

"I haven't seen him for ages," he said. "Why do you want to know?"

"Ask no questions, catch no flies!" said Slubble-jum. Some of the other nethercats sniggered, and he turned on them.

"Get back to your work!" he snapped. "It's only a miserable yuman boy. Not worth wasting your time over. And as for you," he added to Toby, "I'll give you a fair choice. Either you can walk the plank now and swim for it later, or you can be my cabin boy now and walk the plank later."

"I'd rather not walk the plank at all, if you don't mind," said Toby. Most of the other nethercats had moved away, but one had stayed behind – a big one with a mean expression and coppery scales that made him look like the nethercat equivalent of a ginger tom. He now spoke up.

"Keep 'im if I were you, Cap'n. We could do with another worker, and you never know when an 'ostage might come in useful."

"I suppose you're right, Fattascratch," said Slubblejum. "But why haven't you run up the Jolly Dodger? Fine sort of bosun you are, if you can't even remember a little thing like the flag."

Fattascratch gave the captain a nasty look, but went and pulled a cord attached to the main mast. Toby watched as the black flag was hauled to the top, where it fluttered in the breeze, showing the emblems of a skull and fishbones.

"Well, don't just stand there staring," said Slub-

blejum. "Get on with your work. Idle hands spoil the broth, you know."

"What work, Slubblejum?"

"Scrubbing the deck, of course. And you address me as Sir, don't forget. S-I-R spells Sirrrrr!" The greeney nethercat made a rush towards Toby, who backed away from him and grabbed a bucket and a scrubbing brush that were lying at the foot of the mast. Toby began to make a great show of scrubbing vigorously.

"That's better," said Slubblejum, and went off to the poop deck in the stern of the ship.

There were two small cabins on the main deck, between the tall masts, and also several objects covered with tarpaulins along each side of the

deck. Although Slubblejum was standing on the small raised deck in the stern which served as the captain's bridge, Toby found it was easy enough to get into a position where Slubblejum could not see him. He put down the scrubbing brush, and being nothing if not curious, he peeped under one of the tarpaulins to see what it was covering. It turned out to be a small cannon, looking oddly out of place, somehow. Toby suspected the ship had not been designed as a fighter.

He sat down and made himself comfortable, leaning against the cannon, while he watched the nethercats going about their various tasks. Some of them were adjusting the sails, with Fattascratch

shouting orders at them. One was mending a piece of rope, while another three were working as a fishing team. Two of these had dived overboard, and after a while they would come back with one or two fishes, which they threw onto the deck. The third member of the team popped the catch into a large bucket, which he took into one of the small cabins when it was full. Toby learned later that the whole crew, including the captain, took it in turns to do this fishing duty. They enjoyed the splash in the sea, and as they ate twice as many raw fish as they brought back to cook, there was no danger of anyone going hungry. Except perhaps the human cabin boy.

One plump, purple nethercat was sitting in the middle of the deck peeling potatoes, which Toby took as a good sign. There must be chips on the menu as well as fish. However, he felt a bit conspicuous sitting where the purple nethercat could see him, so he got up and slipped round to the far side of the cannon, facing out to sea. He made himself comfortable again, and sat watching the sparkling waves, and listening to the seagulls crying overhead. He murmured to himself,

"Might as well enjoy life on the ocean wave. But fancy Slubblejum becoming a pirate!" A small voice replied from somewhere nearby,

"A pirate who sailed on the ocean
Was asked why he drank shaving lotion.
He said, 'Drinking rum
Just unsettles my tum,
When the ship on the ocean's in motion.'"

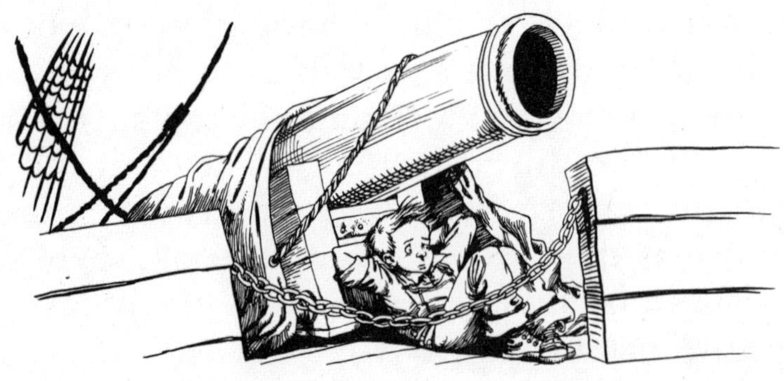

Chapter 3 ~ Stowaway

Toby was startled by the voice, which sounded just like his old friend the chameleon. There was no one to be seen, but that only proved the point, as he was an expert at blending in with the background.

"Hardly Visible!" exclaimed Toby. "Is that really you? It's great not to see you again."

"Shhhhh!" said an urgent whisper. "Don't give me away. I'm a stowaway."

"Sorry," said Toby, lowering his voice. "But that should just suit you, with your gift for keeping hidden."

"That's what you think," squeaked the chameleon. "Are there any nethercats watching?"

When Toby said not at the moment, a bump appeared at the front end of the tarpaulin, then something popped out onto the deck. It was the familiar chameleon shape, but instead of being well camouflaged, it was a bright tangerine colour that clashed with everything around it.

"What are you playing at?" demanded Toby. "Why are you that silly colour?"

"I can't help it," said the chameleon. "I've got stuck. No matter how hard I try, I can't change to another colour. I've been hiding in the cannon's mouth – I hope I get fair warning if they decide to use it."

"What a problem!" said Toby. "And Slubble-jum seems very interested in chameleons for some reason. Well, we'll have to call you Highly Visible from now on. Or Hardly Suitable."

"Never mind calling me names!" squeaked the chameleon indignantly. "It's not funny, I assure you. That is why I've stowed away on the ship. I have to find my way to the Middle Land, wher-ever that is." Then he told Toby the whole story.

Long, long, ago, when the world was full of strange things like dinosaurs and dodos, all the chameleons lived in the heart of the Middle Land. They were very shy and timid, because they were bright tangerine in colour, and so were an easy prey for all the terror-dactyls and such-like that roamed the earth at that time. So, generation after generation, they hid themselves in the shade of a great and mysterious tree that grew in the heart of a hidden valley.

The tree's trunk was like glass, and its leaves were like living diamonds glinting in the light of the sun. It was so beautiful that whenever some fierce animal wandered into the valley, the animal would be completely fascinated by the tree, and not even notice the little chameleons. So they were able to live there in peace for many centuries.

At last, however, the valley, big as it was, grew so overcrowded that you could hardly move for chameleons. Some of the more adventurous ones decided to move out. But as they did so, they made a strange discovery. They found that they were no longer tangerine, but took on the colour of whatever was nearest to them. They realized that they had absorbed some of the power of the great tree, and that it would keep them hidden from the bigger animals wherever they went.

After that, of course, the chameleons spread all over the world, and the great tree became just a legend to them. But they passed on the message to their children that they should never eat tangerines, because if they did, they might turn tangerine colour again. If that happened, the only cure would be to return to the Middle Land and absorb some of the rays from the great tree.

"Well, that's what happened to me," concluded Hardly Visible ruefully. "I admit I was Hardly Sensible, and I discovered that I don't even like tangerines, but I couldn't resist trying one just because it was forbidden. So here we are.

"In modern times, now that chameleons have learned something about science, we know it is in fact the Prism Tree. All the colours on earth depend on it. It catches the light from the sun, and breaks it up into different colours for the rest of the world. There is a famous rhyme about it:

In deepest heart of Middle Land
The mighty Prism Tree doth stand;
No colour has that tree so bright,
All colours shimmer from its light.

But when the ancient dragon's seen,
With eyes of blue and feathers green,
And scales that shine but change no more,
Make haste – the Prism Tree restore!

I don't know what the last bit means, but I don't suppose it matters. The thing is, I have to find the Middle Land, before I get eaten by a terror-dactyl, or a nethercat, or something."

"Do you know where this Middle Land is?" asked Toby.

"All I know is that I feel something tugging at me, here, in my chest. I think I must be like a homing pigeon where the Prism Tree is concerned. I mean, I wouldn't know how to find it on a map, but I know when I am going in the right direction. It just feels right, somehow."

Toby and Hardly Visible were so busy thinking about the Prism Tree that neither of them noticed that Slubblejum had left the poop deck. He had a suspicion that Toby was not getting on with his work, and had come looking for him. As the nethercat crept round the side of the cannon, he saws the small tangerine object, made a sudden pounce, and caught it firmly in one webbed paw.

"Well, well, and what have we here?' he exclaimed. "A cuckoo among the pigeons!"

"Ouch!" said Hardly Visible, as the nethercat squeezed a bit too tight. Slubblejum turned on Toby with a hiss.

"What a lying little yuman you are! I knew you were hand in mouth with that chamelyeron."

"I never . . ." began Toby, but Slubblejum was not listening.

"Come now, my little chamelyeron," he was saying. "I've been looking everywhere for someone like you. Just think how useful it would be if we nethercats could change colour. We could creep up on the yumans and . . . Nethercats rule, OK? So *you* are now going to turn a nice shade of green, and explain exactly how you do it, step by step. Or else. Do I make myself clear?"

"But I can't!" squeaked Hardly Visible.

"No such thing as Can't," said Slubblejum. "Won't is more like it."

"It's true,' said Toby. "He can't change colour, honestly. He's got stuck."

"Yes, that's right," said Hardly, nodding his head vigorously. "That's why I am on your ship – to get to the Middle Land and find the cure."

"Aha!" said Slubblejum. "So there is a cure. And if something can make *you* change colour again, why shouldn't it make *me* change colour as well? And the rest of my gallant band.”

The rest of the gallant band were gathering around to see what the commotion was about, and they supported Slubblejum with various cries of, “Hear, hear!” and “You tell him, Cap’n!”

Hardly Visible realized he had said the wrong thing.

“I don’t know anything,” he said. “I mean, I was just hoping there *might* be a cure.”

“Scratchy!” said Slubblejum suddenly. “Prepare a torture chamber. A *small* torture chamber.”

“A t-t-t . . .” said Hardly Visible.

“There’s no need for that, Cap’n,” said the big, ginger nethercat, pushing his way to the front of the crowd. He flexed his claws, which were very long and sharp, and then grinned, showing a fine set of teeth. “I’ll just fight ’im tooth and nail, as the saying goes.” The other nethercats laughed.

“Eeeeeek!” said Hardly Visible. Then, in a quick gabble, before Fattascratch could come anywhere near him, he told the whole story of the Prism Tree. As he spoke, however, the nethercats’ grins gradually gave way to scowls.

“That’s no use to us, Cap’n,” said Fattascratch. “We can’t just sit down for humpteen generations in the shade of that there tree.”

“I know that, stupid!” said Slubblejum. He threw Hardly Visible down in disgust, and the much relieved chameleon scuttled away out of sight. "We'll just have to think of something else, won't we? Now get back to work, all of you. Especially you," he added, turning on Toby. "I Want This Deck Scrubbed. Now. Understand?"

After that, Toby had no choice but to get back to work. It was no easy task, as the deck heaved and rolled all the time, the bucket kept sliding about, and a few times Toby lost his balance and slipped on the wet surface. After about an hour of this he ached all over, and was feeling rather seasick again.

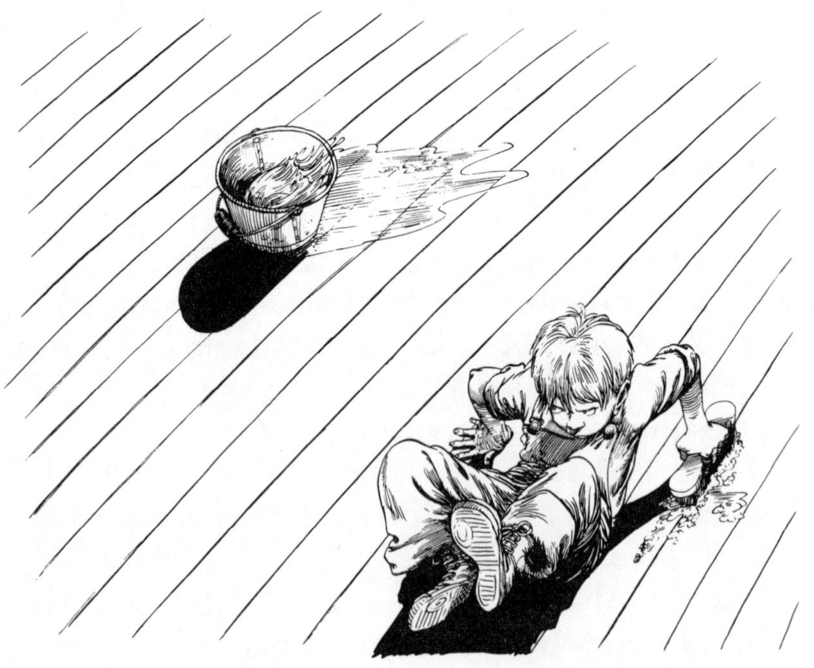

Fortunately, there was then an interruption. Plates of fish and chips were being handed out to the crew from one of the small cabins on deck, which was evidently the cook's galley. The waiter was a young, nervous looking nethercat with pale yellow scales. Toby had noticed that he seemed to spend half his life hiding from Slubblejum, and the other half hiding from Fattascratch, and he had mentally nicknamed him Scaredy-cat.

"W-w-welcome a-b-board," whispered the yellow one, as he handed Toby his plate. "Just d-d-do what they say, and they'll f-f-f-feed you all right." Then he scampered back to the galley as if afraid of being punished for speaking at all.

Toby sat down with his plate, but was feeling too sick to eat, unlike the nethercats, who finished their meal in about three minutes flat. Then most of them disappeared below decks, apart from the look-out high on the main mast, and a thin, silvery one at the wheel. Toby threw his food overboard, causing a lot of screaming and swooping among the seagulls that were following the ship. It was beginning to get dark, and no one had said anything about where he could sleep, but it was obviously going to be too cold to stay on deck. He followed the last of the nethercats down the hatch.

He passed a couple of doors behind which he

could hear nethercat voices, then found that the next door led to a large hold full of everything under the sun. Besides good stores like sacks of potatoes and tins of dried milk, there were piles of ropes, old buckets, pans with and without handles, a canvas sail waiting to be mended, and a whole carpenter's shop of saws and drills, hammers and boxes of nails. In one corner, beside a row of big wooden boxes marked *Cannon Balls*, he found a pile of empty potato sacks.

"This looks quite cosy," he said to Hardly Visible, who had followed him down, and was now scuttling around, poking his small nose into everything.

As he curled up among the sacks, he heard a small squeaky voice:

> *"A llama who lived in Brazil*
> *Wore pyjamas to keep out the chill.*
> *A tourist said, 'Wow!*
> *Can that be a cow,*
> *Or am I just terribly ill?"'*

Chapter 4 ~ A Dastardly Plot

Toby tossed and turned for a long time in the strange surroundings. Eventually, however, he fell asleep, and it seemed like only two minutes later that he was woken abruptly by a couple of nethercats coming into the hold to look for some rope.

"Just look at the sleepy head!" remarked one of them.

"Better be quick, or you'll miss your breakfast," added the other.

Toby suddenly felt ravenous. He had quite got over his seasickness, and the ship was, in fact, moving much more gently than the previous day as the weather had turned calmer. Breakfast turned out to be a bowl of porridge, which Toby had to eat by the nethercat method of lapping it up with his tongue, as there were no spoons. The porridge was the sweet and milky kind, and he realized that the nethercats, like ordinary cats, loved anything with milk in it, even though they had to use dried milk on board ship.

He had barely finished eating, however, when Slubblejum came along, pushed a couple of rags and some brass polish into Toby's hand, and said he wanted all the brass fittings polished until he could see his face in them.

Funny how he's suddenly decided to smarten up the ship as soon as I've come along, reflected Toby. The brass handles on the cabin doors had obviously not been cleaned for a long time, and it was a dreadful task to get them clean. He moved on to a brass rail near the poop deck, where, as usual, a thin, silvery nethercat was at the wheel. Toby was to learn later that his full name was Finkleweed, although he was usually known as Weedy.

Finkleweed was a melancholy soul, and his heart was not really in this pirating business. As the ship was rather under-manned (or under-nethercatted), he had to take the dog watch and the cat watch and most of the other watches in between. He used to relieve the boredom by talking to himself, and as Toby worked he heard the nethercat reciting:

*"There was an old woman who lived long ago,
This story's so sad that I want you to know . . .*

*There was an old woman who lived ago long,
There's nothing so sad as this terrible song . . .*

*There was an old woman in days long gone by,
This story's so sad I keep wanting to cry . . .*

*There was an old woman in long ago years,
This story's so sad that I keep shedding tears . . .*

*There was an old woman in ages of yore,
This story's so sad I can't tell any more . . ."*

Finkleweed heaved a great sigh, and fell silent. "Is that it?" asked Toby, looking up in surprise. He got no answer, because Slubblejum turned up at that moment, demanding to know why Toby was distracting the pilot in the course of his duty.

"Little pitchers make most noise, that's the trouble," added Slubblejum. "Get below decks and clean the hold. And don't let me see your face for another hour, do you hear?"

Toby reluctantly went below decks, fed up with being ordered about. He wandered around, satisfying his curiosity about the parts of the ship he had not yet seen. First he found a couple of private cabins, presumably belonging to Slubblejum and Bosun Fattascratch, then a bigger room containing only piles of straw where the rest of the nethercats slept at night. That reminded him that he had not slept much himself. He would very much like a little snooze, but it was too stuffy below decks during the day, and he decided to go back up for some fresh air.

He cautiously climbed the steep wooden steps, taking care that no one was watching, then slipped under a tarpaulin, next to one of the cannons. He arranged the tarpaulin with a little gap on the seaward side, so that he could breathe easily without the danger of being seen. He was just beginning to nod off when he heard voices nearby. At first he just curled up and tried to shut them out, but then he heard something that made him stop feeling at all sleepy. He froze, hardly daring to breathe for fear of being discovered.

It was Slubblejum who was speaking. He had
gathered the nethercats together, and sent someone, apparently the young Scaredy-cat, to take
over the wheel from Finkleweed for a while.

"Now, is everyone else here?" said Slubblejum.
He started counting heads, "Bogglewick, Clatter-
claws, Snozzletwitch, Fattascratch, Nobblegood,
Paddywack, Hoggleblock, Slobbershrimp, Feckle-
foot, Worraglump . . . Ah, there you are, Finkleweed – Well, I've just had a brilliant idea!"

He waited for the nethercats to clap, but as no one was going to applaud until they heard what the great idea was, he continued.

"I don't really see much future in this pirating business. It's not as if we lived in the days of the Spanish Armadillo."

"True," murmured several voices.

"But opportunity knocks for him who waits, and now's our chance. There's a French proverb . . ."

"Oh, no!" said someone.

"Pssssss!" spat Slubblejum. "Listen, and you may learn something. *La nuit, tous les chats sont gris.* I know that's right, because I have just looked it up. And for the benefit of the uneducated, it means all cats are grey at night. Well, that's the answer."

Dead silence greeted this remark. Slubblejum gave a big sigh. Sometimes the stupidity of his fellow nethercats amazed him.

"Listen,' he said. "Why have we been looking everywhere for a chamelyeron?"

"To teach us how to change colour," said someone.

"Exactly," said Slubblejum. "And why do we want to be able to change colour?"

"So that we can creep up on yumans without being noticed," said the same voice.

"Well done, Worraglump," said Slubblejum sarcastically. "Go to the top of the class. Well, don't you see? If we cut down that old Prism Tree, there will be no more colours in the world. Just imagine it – a grey, misty twilight all the time, and the nethercats will just be darker shadows in a shadowy world.

"You want some nice yuman food? Just slip in and take it. You want some clever yuman invention? Help yourself! We'll have micro-ovens, food processors, electric blankets – every comfort you could desire. Even motor cars. Just imagine Scratchy in a Rolls Royce! And the yumans will never suspect us. They will be so busy blaming each other and starting fights amongst themselves that we will be able to go where we like and do what we like. Before long, it will be nethercats, not yumans, that are the top dogs on this planet. If you know what I mean."

Slubblejum's last sentence was drowned in an outburst of clapping and cheering, as light finally dawned on the nethercats. Toby was nearly deafened for a couple of minutes, until Slubblejum managed to call them to order.

"Now listen," he said. "When I caught the chamelyeron, he was just saying something about finding the Prism Tree like a homing pigeon. So once we get to land, he can lead us straight to it. All we have to do is convince him and that boy that we are their friends, and want to help them."

He must think we're both daft, thought Toby.

"Meanwhile, it's up to you, Weedy, to find this Middle Land on your maps, and make sure we are sailing in the right direction. Then, when we reach land, some of us will kindly escort our little friends until we find the tree, and Slub's your uncle!"

"Brilliant, Cap'n!" said someone. Slubblejum purred, then decided it was time they all got back to work. "And just remember to be nice to our guests!" was his final remark, as Toby heard the nethercats moving away.

Toby was feeling stunned with shock. For a few minutes he couldn't move, but just sat there, thinking of what the world would be like if all the colours were destroyed. He shuddered, as if an icy wind had blown over him. He thought of grey trees, grey flowers, grey butterflies. Everything always the same, like living in a November fog forever, without any hope of spring ever coming again. And he was the only one who could prevent it – with the help of a chameleon-gone-wrong, who couldn't even change his own colour. He suddenly felt very small, and very much alone.

Chapter 5 ~ Duck's Ditty

Toby managed to slip back down to the hold without being seen. There he met Hardly Visible and told him what he had overheard. They agreed that as soon as they reached land they would have to give Slubblejum the slip, and try to get help somehow.

"We'll just have to play it by ear," said Toby. "Look out, here comes Slubblejum." The chameleon dived into a dark corner. Slubblejum was full of smiles, and carrying a large map.

"Well, my little man," he said to Toby, who winced. He hated being called a little man by anyone, especially nethercats.

"You will be glad to hear that we have managed to find out where the Middle Land is. The Prism Tree cannot help *us* to change colour, but to show we bear no grudges, we have decided to help you and your little friend on your way. Now, this is what we have discovered." He spread out the map near a porthole. It was a very old one, on yellow parchment curling up at the edges. "This place called Cathay is where we should be heading for." He pronounced it Cat-hay.

"Never heard of it," said Toby. This map's a bit old, isn't it? Do you think . . ."

"Perfectly good map!" interrupted Slubblejum. "But the point is that Cat-hay has another name. Look, it's here, in the margin. Well, what do you think of that, eh?"

Toby looked where Slubblejum's claw was pointing, and gasped.

"That's right!" said Slubblejum triumphantly. "*The Middle Kingdom*! There is no doubt about it, this Cat-hay place is where you will find the Prism Tree, as sure as eggs is fried. We have changed our course, and we are now heading for Cat-hay full speed ahead. There now, what do you think of that?"

"Oh, thank you, Slub . . . Sir," said Toby, with as much enthusiasm as he could manage. "That *is* kind of you."

Slubblejum smirked, and told Toby he should come up out of the stuffy old hold, and that he needn't do any more cleaning today if he was tired. Why didn't he just sit on deck for a while, and invite his dear little tangerine friend to join him? He was sure they had not meant to frighten him yesterday . . .

The next few days would have been like a holiday for Toby, if he had not been so anxious about the Prism Tree. Occasionally Slubblejum forgot to be nice, and made him do some work, but mostly he just sat around enjoying the sea breeze and talking to Hardly Visible, who felt safe enough to come out of hiding.

Toby expected the rest of the voyage, to go on in this uneventful way, but there was one more unusual incident before they reached land. It happened after twenty-four hours of very high winds, which had tossed the ship about roughly, and brought Toby's seasickness back. In the evening, however, the wind had dropped, and Toby and Hardly Visible were sitting out on the deck, enjoying the calm after the storm.

Toby had not seen any seagulls since soon after boarding the *Catty Sark*, so he looked up in excitement when he heard their raucous cries again. He knew it was a sign they were nearing land once more. One of the seagulls was an unusual speckled brown colour, and it flapped its wings more clumsily than the others. Then he realized it was not a seagull at all, but a duck, and it seemed to be in trouble. As he watched, it fluttered feebly, then fell onto the deck, where it lay gasping for breath, and apparently exhausted.

Toby went over to have a look at it, and arrived at the same time as Slubblejum. The nethercat's green eyes lit up.

"Aha!" he said. "All we need now is orange sauce. I just fancy a nice roast duck for tomorrow's dinner."

"No you don't!" said Toby, grabbing the duck and tucking it under his arm. "That's *my* duck. I got here first."

Slubblejum hesitated. It was obvious that a struggle was going on inside him, as he badly wanted the duck, but he didn't want to upset Toby at this stage.

"Very well," he said at last. "But remember – when you cook it, I want some. One man's goose is another man's gander, you know." Then he went off and left them in peace. The duck was trembling all over.

"Was that a cat?" she quacked as Toby put her down. He explained that it was a nethercat, and that the ship was on her way to Cathay.

"That's strange," said the duck. "I think that's an old name for China, where I come from. Perhaps I'm back on the track after all. I'm a Mandarin duck, as you may have noticed. That's the highest class of ducks, you know." She spread out her wings to show the dark green wing tips, and Toby noticed the elegant white stripe around her eyes. "But, please, is there something to eat and drink?" she added. "It has been days since I had anything."

Toby went to fetch a bowl of water and some ship's biscuits, which he had discovered tended to be rather wormy. The duck was delighted.

"Thanks, thanks!" she said. "My name's Dee Lee, by the way. At least, that's the English version – we put our surnames first, really. Anyway, I've been having such a dreadful time ..." Then, in between having a good feed, she told Toby and Hardly Visible her whole story.

A few weeks ago she had met a wonderful Mandarin drake called Dah Lee. He was so handsome with his bright colours – black and white and green and orange – and had a fine character to match. They had fallen in love at first sight, and got married without more ado.

Before looking for a permanent home, they had decided to go for their honeymoon to a nearby small country in a beautiful mountain region. It was called Nos Mo King, and the happy couple had stayed near the Emperor's palace, which was one of the great wonders of the world.

While they were there, however, a terrible thing had happened. The Emperor kept a nightingale in a cage, and it was his pride and joy. But one day a careless servant had left the cage door open, and it had escaped. The terrified servant had noticed the brightly coloured Dah Lee, and had put him in the cage to replace the nightingale. The Emperor was pleased with the drake, but did not like his voice very much, so Dah Lee was told he must learn to sing like a nightingale within a month, or his head would be cut off.

Dah Lee's poor wife, left alone in a strange land, had started to fly back to China to get help from her friends, but she had been blown off course by a gale, and had found herself over the sea. One week had gone by already, and she was at her wits' end wondering how to help her husband to escape, or at least to learn to sing like a nightingale, before the time ran out.

"Well, Dilly – I mean Dee Lee," said Toby as she finished, "I wish we could help you. But we have a big problem of our own." He told her all about the Prism Tree, and finally said, "It sounds as though Dah Lee will be safe for three weeks. Why don't you come with us to get help for the Prism Tree first? We just can't risk going off to Nos Mo King and perhaps letting the nethercats find the tree first. They are cunning, you know, and they can travel pretty fast. But as soon as we have solved that problem, we will both go with you to rescue Dah Lee. How will that do?"

Dee Lee reluctantly agreed, though it was obvious that she would rather rescue her husband first, and worry about whether the world was going to be penny plain or twopence coloured afterwards. But now it was time to go below decks to bed. Toby settled the duck on a potato sack, then curled up in his own usual ones. He set his alarm watch for the morning, and then made it chime *Jingle Bells*, as he usually did at night. It made him feel more at home, somehow. Almost before it had stopped he fell asleep, and dreamed of ducks and dragons, prisms and palaces, watches and water-lilies, all mixed up together.

Chapter 6 ~ A Dragon in a Dudgeon

Next morning, as they were sitting on the deck having their breakfast, Hardly Visible was in a poetical mood – or rather, he had decided to show off in front of the duck. After seven or eight limericks, most of which Toby had heard before, Dee Lee interrupted him with, "It's my turn now," and recited,

> *"There was a chameleon called Hardly Visible,*
> *Who was always reciting poems,*
> *But he fell in the sea*
> *And was drowned like a flea,*
> *And the poems got eaten by a whale."*

Hardly gave an indignant squeak, and Toby said, "It's suppose to rhyme, you know."

"It does," said Dee Lee. "Well, some of it does."

The chameleon, determined to have the last word, said,

> *"There was an old writer called Lear,*
> *Whose poems were exceedingly queer,*
> *For he never found time*
> *To work out the last rhyme,*
> *That nonsensical writer called –*
>   Land Ahoy!"

"Called Land Ahoy!" exclaimed Toby. "What on earth are you talking about?"

"Land Ahoy!" shouted Hardly Visible again, and the cry was taken up by the nethercat lookout, from his position on the main mast. It was indeed land coming into sight at last.

They spent the next hour or so watching excitedly as the shore line grew from just a shadow on the horizon to a great bay lined with dark cliffs. Toby gathered from the nethercats' talk that they intended to follow the shore until they came to the mouth of a big river marked on their map as the Oki Koki. They would anchor the ship there, then make their way overland in search of Cathay.

At present they were sailing towards a headland at the east of the bay, which jutted out quite a long way from the rest of the shore. The nethercats all seemed to be fully occupied in steering or adjusting the sails. Toby saw his opportunity.

"Can you both swim?" he whispered to the others, then said, "Sorry!" to Dee Lee, who

squawked indignantly. Hardly Visible climbed onto Toby's shoulder, and said he would rather let him do the swimming, if he didn't mind. For another few minutes, they stood by the deck rail, partly hidden by the cannons, as if they were just admiring the view. Then, as the ship came opposite the headland, Toby glanced round to make sure that no nethercats were looking their way.

"Now!" he hissed, and slipped down into the sea, letting the current carry him to the wake of the ship. It only needed a few minutes' hard swimming to bring Toby to the nearest part of the beach. Even as he fell gasping onto the sand, the *Catty Sark* rounded the headland and was lost to sight. Dee Lee, seeing that the coast was clear, stopped her frantic paddling up and down the waves, and flew the rest of the way. Then all three sat for a few minutes on the sand to get their breath back.

"Come on!" said Toby. "We'd better get moving before the nethercats start looking for us." They set off running along the beach, away from the direction the ship had gone, but soon slowed to a walking pace as they discovered there was no way up the steep cliffs. There was nothing for it but to keep trudging on over the sand and rocks. It must have been about an hour before they got round another small headland and saw another, almost identical, beach ahead of them.

"The tide's coming in," said Toby. "I hope we're not going to get trapped." Then he noticed a large cave in the cliffs ahead of them, and started to move towards it.

"Hey, where are you going?" squeaked Hardly Visible from Toby's shoulder. "We haven't time for exploring caves." However, Toby was known at school as Curiosity Jones, and there was no way he was going to miss seeing what was in that cave. As they reached the entrance, Hardly Visible said,

> *"There once was a man who said, 'There*
> *Is a cave I'll explore for a dare.'*
> *What he found no one knows,*
> *But they rescued his toes,*
> *And a very nice lock of his hair."*

They stood just inside the cave mouth, letting their eyes gets used to the darkness.

"I don't like it," said Dee Lee. "It's nasty and black at the back."

They all jumped with fright as something in the shadows said, "Good morning – as the saying goes."

Dee Lee squawked and Hardly Visible squeaked, and they both ran back out of the cave at top speed. Toby seemed frozen to the spot, but his eyes were getting used to the dimness, and he could now make out the shape of a large animal. It was lying at the back of the cave with its head on the ground between its front paws, breathing a rather smoky breath. It had great, leathery wings, and a long tail which ended in a point like an arrow head. In fact, it looked like all the pictures he had ever seen of dragons.

Toby took a deep breath, and managed to say, "Er . . . How do you do?"

"I don't do at all," said the dragon. "That's the trouble."

"Is something the matter?" asked Toby.

"Everything's the matter," replied the dragon. "I'm in a dudgeon, that's what."

"Don't you mean a dungeon?" asked Toby, looking round the cave. "Have you got a cold?"

"No, I mean a dudgeon, not a dudgeon," said

the dragon. "Oh dear, now I ab gettig a code. Aaaaatishooooo!" He let out a sneeze that blew Toby flat on his back in the sand. Toby picked himself up, and moved to a safer distance.

"It's all your fault," said the dragon. "for thinkig aboud codes – please stop is ad once. Aaaaa . . ." Toby ducked, and the sneeze went over his head this time.

"I don't see what difference it makes what *I* think," he said, as he cautiously straightened up again.

"It's all ibagination," said the dragon. "I'll tell you aboud id, but please do stop thinkig of codes, or I won't be able to tell you anythig."

"Well, I'll try," said Toby, and he made a great effort to think about sunny days and being in the best of health.

"That's better!" said the dragon, and he began to tell his tale:

> *"It's awful to be mythical –*
> *it isn't nice at all*
> *When you're neither bright nor beautiful*
> *and neither big nor small;*
> *I can't breathe fire to show my ire,*
> *it's really a disgrace,*
> *Or face the whole thing calmly*
> *when I haven't any face!*

It's awful to be mythical,
*   it makes me very sad,*
And what is even worse is that
*   I'm mythically bad –*
I have a reputation
*   I eat maidens for a treat,*
But it's all imagination,
*   for I never even eat!*

It's awful to be mythical,
*   it really isn't fair;*
I can't go for a walk because
*   I'm neither here nor there,*
I can't invite another friendly
*   dragon home for tea,*
For there aren't such things as dragons,
*   so there isn't even me!"*

"Of course there are such things as dragons!" said Toby. "At least, I *think* there are." The dragon looked very relieved at this. "And if you think you have problems," added Toby, "just look at the fix we are in."

By this time curiosity had got the better of his small companions' fears, and they had crept back to listen. Toby told the dragon about the Prism Tree, and the duck added her own story. Then Hardly Visible said,

"A dragon called Fiery Fred
Had buckets of coal in his head,
But the neighbours complained
When he breathed fire and flames,
So he used smokeless fuel instead,"

which they all agreed was quite irrelevant.

"I know!" said Toby suddenly. "You could give us a lift. Hardly Visible can tell you the right way to go. He feels it in his chest."

"Well, I don't know," said the dragon reluctantly. "It's a bit of a risk, you know."

"What risk?" demanded Toby. "It seems safe enough to me. And once we find the Prism Tree," he added as another thought struck him, "you could help us to defend it from the nethercats. I mean, you could breathe fire at them and frighten them away, couldn't you?"

"If you say so," said the dragon.

"Well, that's settled, then," said Toby. "Prism Tree, here we come."

"And then to Nos Mo King," said Dee Lee anxiously.

"Okay," said Toby. "We haven't forgotten."

"Well, I'll do my best," said the dragon. He slithered out of the cave, blinking his red eyes in the sunlight. Then he stretched out his tough, leathery wings, and flapped them slowly.

"Bit stiff," he complained. "I haven't given anyone a lift for centuries. But don't worry – with a good pilot it should come back to me."

Toby climbed up the dragon's side, finding that his scales were bumpy enough to provide plenty of footholds. Hardly Visible hesitated for a moment, then scampered up after him, while Dee Lee flew up the easy way. The dragon took a short run along the sandy beach, and then they were away, soaring off into the blue sky.

Chapter 7 ~ Coo Par Tee

"Ouch!" said Toby as they rose into the air. "I need a cushion. Why have you got so many spikes on your back?"

"It's traditional," said the dragon. "But perhaps if you don't think so much about the spikes, they will go away.'

Toby did not have much success at this, and he soon found that sitting on the dragon's back was not only uncomfortable, it was also rather cold and draughty. And the higher they went, the colder it got. As he was thinking this, the dragon gave a sudden bounce, and climbed higher still.

"Hey, stop!" shouted Toby. "You'll have us falling off if you do things like that."

"Well, you're not helping at all," complained the dragon. "If you want to fly high, think high; if you want to stay low, think low – that's the way it works."

It sounded a funny way of steering to Toby, but he looked down at the patchwork of green and yellow fields below, and tried to think of flying very close to them. The dragon lurched downwards again, giving them all a funny feeling like going down in a lift.

This is ridiculous! thought Toby. *Whatever am I doing? Surely I can't really be flying on the back of a dragon – I must be dreaming.*

Then a strange thing happened. He heard a kind of hissing noise, like the air being let out of a large balloon, and the dragon suddenly shrank to about half his previous size.

"Oh, help!' said Toby out loud. "I do believe in dragons, really I do! Come on, Hardly and Dee Lee – you know that dragons are real, don't you?" And he hung on to the dwindling dragon for dear life.

"Wrrrreeeeooooouuuu! Yow-ow-ow-ow-ow-ow-owoooo!"

That was Slubblejum's reaction when he discovered that Toby and the chameleon were missing. The nethercats had sailed to the mouth of the Oki Koki, then, finding that the river was broad and navigable, they had continued a little way upstream. It was only when they had decided to moor the ship in a wide valley with a patchwork of green and yellow fields, that they had realized that their passengers had disappeared.

When Slubblejum stopped howling to draw his breath, Fattascratch at last managed to get a word in. He pointed out that perhaps the chameleon was not such a great loss after all.

"No use looking for 'em now," he said. "They could be anywhere."

"That's what I've been telling you!" said Slubblejum, who had not said a rational word so far. "Like looking for a four-leaved clover in a haystack."

"But we can manage without 'em," said Fattascratch. "All we got to do is 'ead for the middle of this Cat-Hay place, and ask about the tree as we go along. Somebody must know where it is — stands to reason, don't it?"

Slubblejum recovered his good humour as suddenly as he had lost it. "You're dead right,

Scratchy!" he said, slapping the bosun on the back. "That's just what we'll do. Better travel hopefully than to sit on the fence, I always say. You can stay here and mind the ship."

"But Cap'n . . ." protested Fattascratch, who was looking forward to the trip.

"And you two stay with him," went on Slubble-jum, ignoring him. He pointed to the young one Toby had named Scaredy-Cat, who groaned at the thought of being left with the bullying bosun, and the fat, purple cook. "No time for cooking on this trip," he said. "Strictly emergency rations from now on." The purple one tried not to grin. He always did prefer a quiet life.

The remaining crew members were to go with Slubblejum. He picked up his cutlass, and told the ship's carpenter, a battered-looking nethercat with ragged ears, to provide the others with saws and axes and anything that might be useful.

"If that tree is millions of years old, it must be pretty big," he said. "But the bigger they comes, the harder they falls, eh lads?"

The brightly-coloured group of nethercats looked like some kind of carnival as they set off across the fields. As Fattascratch watched them go, he relieved his bad temper by cuffing young Scaredy-cat round the ears, and telling him to start spring-cleaning the ship and look sharp about it.

The nethercats had been jogging along for about ten minutes when Slubblejum noticed a large bird on the horizon. Or was it a bat? Or a helicopter, perhaps? No, helicopters did not flap their wings like that.

"What do you make of that, Weedy?" he asked.

"Dragon," said Finkleweed briefly.

"Why, so it is," said Slubblejum as it came nearer. "Rather a small one, but definitely a dragon."

"Dangerous things, dragons," said Finkleweed gloomily.

The whole group of nethercats had now stopped and were staring up at the sky.

"It's not such a small dragon," said one.

"Quite a big dragon," agree another, "and getting bigger all the time."

"A big, strong dragon," said Finkleweed. "Very dangerous!"

"What has it got on its back?" demanded Slubblejum as the dragon swooped low over their heads. "Well, of all the cheek! It's that ob-nock-shuss little yuman! And you may be sure he has the chamelyeron with him, not to mention my Sunday dinner!" He was obviously going to have another tantrum, but the other nethercats started moving again.

"Come on, Cap'n," said Finkleweed. "We can't do anything about it except keep moving."

"True," said Slubblejum. "No use taking the horse to water after the door is bolted. Right, lads – follow that dragon!" As the rest of the nethercats were already doing just that, he was wasting his breath.

The dragon itself suddenly seemed as big and powerful as a jet plane. Toby now had no trouble in staying on its broad, smooth back. As the nethercats faded into the distance, the countryside began to whizz beneath them so fast that he hadn't time to see any details. He just got an impression of fields and trees, a broad green plain with a river winding through it, some wooded slopes, a small town or village here and there, then a stretch of open country with lots of sheep grazing on it.

After about an hour of this, there appeared in the distance, ahead of them, a range of mighty snow-capped mountains. Toby was just wondering if they would fly right over the mountains, when the dragon began to slow down. Beneath them, among the foothills, was a large town or city. As they approached, they could see on their left a large and beautiful building standing on a hill by itself. It had dozens of spires and domes that glinted in the sunlight as if they were made of solid gold. The hill on which it stood was laid out as gardens and parkland, and it was surrounded by a high outer wall, which also shone like gold.

"Well, here we are," said the dragon as they reached the outskirts of the town. "This is Coo Par Tee, the capital of Nos Mo King, and you see before you the Emperor's palace, one of the great wonders of the eastern world."

"But we're supposed to be going to Cathay!" exclaimed Toby in dismay.

"The Middle Land!" echoed Hardly Visible.

"I really couldn't help it," said the dragon apologetically. "It was in the air waves – couldn't you feel it? It was saying,

> *"The palace of Coo Par Tee,*
> *As beautiful as can be –*
> *We've got to get back*
> *As quick as a quack*
> *To the palace of Coo Par Tee!"* "

"As quick as a quack!" exclaimed Toby. He looked accusingly at Dee Lee. "It was you, wasn't it?" If the duck could have blushed, she would have done.

"Well, I couldn't help thinking about Dah Lee, could I?" she said.

The dragon was now flying low over the roof-tops, so that the travellers could see the people coming and going in the streets below. As they flew over a big square, they saw that some kind of festival was going on. A procession was making its way round and round, with people in all kinds of fancy dress. At its head was a huge paper dragon, moving rather bumpily on dozens of pairs of human feet.

As the crowd saw another dragon flying overhead, they started shouting and waving in excitement. Toby could not catch what they were saying, but in fact it meant, "Look, look, a flying dragon! It must be a kite! Yes, yes, a dragon kite. Oh, isn't it beautiful!"

The dragon suddenly became very light and bouncy. It started floating gently on the wind over the rooftops and towards another wooded hill near the one with the palace on it. Here it abruptly twisted round as it was caught by a current of air. Toby and his small companions could not prevent themselves from sliding off onto the slope below. The dragon kite, much lighter without its passengers, was caught up by the wind, and sailed away into the distance, its long, paper tail fluttering merrily in the breeze.

Chapter 8 ~ The Toothsayer

"Well, what are we going to do now?" asked Toby as he picked himself up from where he had landed in the grass. Dee Lee came flapping down from a nearby tree, saying excitedly, "Dah, Dah, Rescue Dah!"

"Yes, but how?" asked Toby. "Where's Hardly Visible?" A small tangerine shape emerged from behind a bush, shaking its head and looking rather dazed. "I never did think much of dragons, personally," he remarked.

"I suppose we may as well head for the palace, now we're so near," said Toby.

"That's the lad!" exclaimed Dee Lee. "Attack, attack!"

"Don't be silly!" said Toby rather snappily. He was feeling bruised all over, and was in no mood for attacking a palace single-handed. "Oh dear, I really don't know what to do. I know grown-ups can be a nuisance, but I do wish we had some wise person to give us advice right now.”

“But we have, there is, you do!” said Dee Lee, flapping up and down in her eagerness. “I'd completely forgotten. Did you see a little house through the trees as we floated down?”

“As we fell down like a ton of bricks, you mean,” said Toby, rubbing his seat.

“Well, when Dah and I were here on our honeymoon, we were told it belongs to the Toothsayer.”

“The who?”

“It's a wise person who can say ‘tooth’ in four hundred and thirty-eight languages, and three thousand, nine hundred and ninety-nine dialects.”

“That's a fat lot of use!” said Toby scornfully.

“But it's not just a question of languages,” said Dee Lee. “They say the Toothsayer knows exactly where each dialect is spoken, and who lives there and all about them.”

“Well, I suppose there's no harm in trying,” said Toby. “I didn't notice any house, but you lead the way, Dee Lee.”

The other two followed the duck as she waddled eagerly through the trees and up the hill. Before long, they came out in a small clearing with a little, pagoda-like house in the middle of it. A silvery stream splashed its way through the

clearing, and in front of the house it had been dammed with rocks to form a pool in which some lotus flowers were growing. In the distance they could see the snow-topped mountains against the blue sky, while nearer at hand, and partly hidden by the trees, they caught a glimpse of the Emperor's gilded palace. They all stopped for a moment to admire the beautiful scene.

A tiny wooden bridge led across the stream to the house, and as they approached it, something got up from beside the lotus pool and ran to meet them with much grunting and snuffling. It was a small, wild pig with black, spiky hair. Although it was quite young, it was beginning to sprout a pair of sharp tusks.

"Yack!" said Dee Lee, and flew off to the safety of the pool, while Hardly Visible hastily climbed up Toby's leg and into his trouser pocket. However, the small pig merely sniffed at Toby curiously, and followed him across the bridge.

A voice called out in a strange language from inside the house, and then there appeared a very small and very wrinkled old woman, who stood in the doorway grinning a toothless grin. She wore a long black dress embroidered with geometric patterns, and had a straw coolie hat perched on top of her straggly gray hair.

"Please, Ma'am," asked Toby politely, "is the Toothsayer at home?"

"Oothy, toothy!" said the old woman. "Of course I'm at home. Where do you think I am, eh? *Beside the lake, beneath the trees, fluttering and dancing in the breeze?*" She gave a loud cackle. "Glad you speak English – it's one of my favourite languages, though Swahili is good for the finer points of philosophy, and Serbo-Croat is better for swearing. Well, what do you want? HEEL, SHEP!" This last remark was to the little pig, who was still sniffing around Toby's ankles.

"I need some advice," said Toby. "You see . . ."

"Advice, is it?" said the Toothsayer. "That's what they all want. Can't use their brains, so they use mine instead. Well, my crunchers may be missing, but I've still got all my wisdom teeth. I say the same to all of them, and that is *If*."

"That is if what?" asked Toby, rather bewildered.

"*If, If, If*," said the Toothsayer. "Don't I make myself clear?

If you can keep your head with nothing in it,
Or balance a banana on your nose;
If you can take a daisy chain and spin it
A hundred times around your little toes;

If you can play a bagpipe filled with treacle,
Or knit yourself a long spaghetti coat;
If you can ballet dance upon a steeple,
Or win the Derby riding on a goat;

If you can stuff a toothpaste tube with thistles,
Or tie your ears together just for fun,
Or eat a sago pudding while you whistle,
You're a better man than I am, Ginger Dunn!

"Have a jelly baby," she added abruptly, pulling a bag from her pocket.

"Oh, thank you," said Toby, who was beginning to feel it was past his lunch time.

"Gum, gum!" mumbled the Toothsayer through a jelly baby. "Mmmm thmmm mmslf

y'nmmmm . . ." She gave a gulp, then repeated, "I make them myself, you know. Always had a sweet tooth, I'm afraid, and now I've no teeth at all. But that's the price you pay. Well, what kind of advice?"

"It's about the Prism Tree," said Toby.

"Not for tourists," said the Toothsayer firmly. "Much too important. Pain in the tooth, these gawpers and gazers, Pah! Crowds of them these days. They are welcome to look at Hullabaloo, or Mount Proppacoppakettle, but not the Prism Tree. Definitely not."

"But we are not tourists," explained Toby. "You see, the three of us . . ."

"What three?" interrupted the Toothsayer. "I can only see one of you, and you're not very big." Toby called out to Dee Lee, who flapped up from the pool, and landed a few yards away, keeping a wary eye on the little pig.

"Oh, *that*'s with you, is it?" said the Toothsayer. "And number three is up your sleeve, I suppose."

"In my pocket, actually," said Toby. "He's called Hardly Visible." The chameleon poked his head out at the sound of his name.

"Don't tell me!" said the Toothsayer. "Been eating tangerines. They all do it. I had Dizzy Peers and Haydn Squeak here just last week. So you want to find the Prism Tree to cure him."

"But it's not only that," said Toby. "We are being followed by a nethercat called Slubblejum and his cronies . . ."

"Never trust a nethercat," put in the Toothsayer.

". . . And they want to cut down the Prism Tree and turn everything grey. We got a lift here on the back of a dragon and . . ."

The Toothsayer suddenly grabbed Toby by the shoulders and looked into his eyes.

"Blue!" she said. "You've got *blue eyes*! And the duck has green wing feathers, and the chameleon can't change his colour. Oh, galloping gumboils! Oh, terrible toothache! The end of the world is upon us. Oh, dent, dant, diente, dente, dens!"

With that, she fell in a heap on the ground and lay completely still.

Chapter 9 ~ From Bad to Worse

Toby was dumbfounded by the Toothsayer's reaction. He bent over her to see if she were alive or dead, while the little pig started snuffling curiously at her face. The Toothsayer sat up suddenly and pushed the pig away.

"Small Hairy Earth Pig, take your nose out of my face!" she shouted, settling the coolie hat on her head again.

"I'm glad you're all right," said Toby. "But why should it be the end of the world? And what has the colour of my eyes to do with it?"

"Zahn, Zahn, Zahn!" exclaimed the Toothsayer. "Sit down and I'll explain. Never stand if you can sit. Conservation of energy, that's the thing."

Toby sat on the grass, and the Toothsayer began to recite the second verse of the Prism Tree poem:

"But when the ancient dragon's seen,
With eyes of blue and feathers green,
And scales that shine but change no more,
Make haste – the Prism Tree restore.

"It has just come true, when you rode on the dragon's back," she explained. "He was seen with eyes of blue – your eyes, not his own – and the duck's green feathers, and the chameleon's scales that cannot change their colour any more. That is the sign we have been waiting for. The Time has come. You must rescue the Prism Tree and save the world."

"But surely it's not the end of the world if everything turns grey?" asked Toby.

Then the Toothsayer explained, with a lot of big words like *chlorophyll* and *photosynthesis*, that all life on earth depends on the sun, and that it is the green part of the plants that absorbs the sunlight. If the plants turned grey they would die. Then all the animals that live on plants would die. And then all the other animals that eat the plant-eating animals would die as well. Before long, the whole animal kingdom would be wiped out. Even in the sea, the fishes depend on plankton that absorbs the sunlight near the surface, just as the land animals depend on plants.

She went on to explain that the Prism Tree was

not the first of its kind, and it would not be the last. The first one had taken root millions of years ago, when the world was very young. Eventually it had been replaced by the present Prism Tree, which was now millions of years old itself. In its prime, nothing could harm or destroy it, but once its days were complete, it could be cut down, though only on a night when there was no moon. Then it must be replaced by a new Prism Tree.

"And so it goes on," she concluded. "And on and on and on and . . . Well, you must go quickly and carry out the instructions in the third verse of the poem."

"We didn't know there was a third verse," said Toby, and the Toothsayer recited,

> *"When no moon shines in darkened sky,*
> *Take one twig from a branch on high;*
> *Where violets grow plant it with care,*
> *And soon new life will blossom there.*

"So all you have to do now is to find the Prism Tree, and plant the cutting on a moonless night. You've done well to have found the Middle Land already."

"What do you mean, found the Middle Land?" asked Toby. "We haven't found Cathay yet."

"What are you talking about?" said the Tooth-sayer. "Well, it's true that old Cathay used to be called the Middle Kingdom, but Nos Mo King is the true centre of the world – where's your etymology?"

"You mean insects?" asked Toby. "I'm rather interested in them."

"No, you toothless wonder! That's *ento*mology. This is where words come from. *Nos* is like *nose*, which is in the middle of your face. *Mo* means world, like the French *monde*. And *King* comes from the same root as the English word *Kingdom* in the Old Language. So *Nos Mo King* means *Middle World Kingdom*. Quite simple really. Now, you had better be on your way."

"But what about my husband?" wailed Dee Lee. Then, of course, she had to tell her own story from the beginning. "We can't just leave him now we are so close," she concluded.

"That's all very well," said the Toothsayer. "But if you don't save the Prism Tree soon, there will be no future for ducks or anyone else either."

At this, Dee Lee set up a most atrocious quacking, so that no one could hear themselves think. Finally, the Toothsayer shouted at the top of her voice,

"Dentists' drills and fearsome fillings! If you don't be quiet, I'll set the pig on you. SHEP!"

The Small Hairy Earth Pig made a rush towards the duck, who flapped up onto the roof of the house, and was at last shocked into silence.

"That's better," said the Toothsayer. "Well, I've just had an idea. I don't think the nethercats will be able to catch you up today, if the dragon was going at full speed. So if you are *very* quick, it won't delay you much to take one of my inventions, and offer it to the Emperor in exchange for Dah Lee. Inventing is my hobby, you know – as well as sweet-making of course.

"Now, what shall it be? The parasol with built-in sprinkler to keep your head cool, or the combined weed-digger and tea-maker, so that you can have tea on the lawn while the machine does the work? No, I don't suppose the Emperor does his own weeding. I know – I'll give him the Walkie-Talkie."

She hobbled back into the house, while the little pig, who was sitting watching them, had a spasm of grunting. Toby could have sworn it was laughing at him. In a couple of minutes the Toothsayer returned, with a small robot trotting at her side. As it reached Toby, its head swivelled round, and a high metallic voice said, "Pleased-to-meet-you-is-there-any-news-have-you-heard-any-good-gossip-recently?"

"It walks the dog and talks to the neighbours," explained the Toothsayer, "so that you can stay in and put your feet up, and then listen to a recording of all the gossip when it comes home. I know the Emperor is fond of dogs, as well as ducks and nightingales and such-like. Come here, Shep, while I demonstrate the dog-walking." The Small Hairy Earth Pig instantly bolted in the opposite direction, and hid behind the house.

"Ticklin' toothpicks!" exclaimed the Toothsayer. "I'll never teach that pig obedience. Never mind – all you do is clip the dog's lead in here, and press this button, and off it goes. You can set the time on this dial for whatever length of walk you want, and then it will turn round and come straight home again. Clever, don't you think? Now, hurry! With any luck you should be back here with Dah Lee within an hour, and while you are gone I will pack a few provisions for your journey."

She started the robot, and it set off at a good speed, with Toby and the others following close behind. Every time the Walkie-Talkie came within a couple of feet of a tree, it would stop and swivel its head round, saying, "Pleased-to-meet-you-is-there-any-news-have-you-heard-any-good-gossip-recently?" They heard the Toothsayer call after them,

"Sorry it can't tell the difference between trees and people yet. I'm working on an improved model, but don't tell the Emperor that."

Chapter 10 ~ A Walk and a Talk

It did not take them long to reach the garden walls surrounding the palace. As Toby was rather small for his age (which always annoyed him), he could barely reach the high brass knocker on the main gate. He just managed it on toptoe, then stood back smartly as there was a creaking of hinges and the gate swung open. It revealed a sturdy gate-keeper in a red and black uniform.

"We have come a long way to see the Great Emperor," said Toby, trying to sound important, "and we have something very interesting to give him."

"Pleased-to-meet-you-is-there-any-news-have-you-heard-any-good-gossip-recently?" said the Walkie-Talkie.

"Hing flang channiwop jessi jossi wim wam," said the gatekeeper

"Oh dear, we never thought of this problem,"

muttered Toby, then said to the gatekeeper, "Please, is there anyone here who speaks English?"

"Nung blogga hollip-juice penka lonki sheraglump," said the gatekeeper. Then he closed the gate firmly in Toby's face.

"Well, that's a good start!" said Toby. He decided it was best to switch off the Walkie-Talkie's voice for the time being. Then a thought struck him, and he asked Dee Lee,

"How is it you speak English, by the way?"

"My mother came from England," said the duck. "She used to say, 'I was born in St James's Park, quactually.' Is St James's Park very beautiful?"

"Well, I'm not a Londoner," said Toby, "but they say . . ." He stopped as the great gate swung open again. This time the gatekeeper had with him a neat little man in green silken robes, who bowed and said,

"Welcome to the Palace of the Exceedingly Honourable Emperor of Nos Mo King. I am the Relatively Honourable Interpreter. Who are you, please?"

"My name is Toby, and this is Dee Lee . . . and Hardly Visible."

"Very Honourable Toe Bee, Dee Lee and No See, please enter," said the Interpreter. He gave a

suspicious look at the small robot as it trotted
through the gate beside them.

"No Foreign Contraptions, please!" he ordered.

"We have brought it for the Emperor," said
Toby. He was about to explain how it worked,
but the Interpreter exclaimed, "Ah, a free and
generous gift. Excellent!" and began to talk about
the palace and the gardens as the huge gate clanged
behind them.

He led the way through a large and beautiful
garden, with peacocks strutting on the well-kept
lawns, and lots of cherry blossoms and willow
trees. In the distance a fountain played in a pool
in front of the gleaming palace itself. When they

reached a wooden seat beside a shrubbery, he invited them to sit down. Toby sat with the duck at his feet, but the chameleon was feeling peckish and went off to look for insects, the dappled sunlight on his tangerine back making him look like some kind of very small tiger in the grass.

"Tell me," said the Interpreter, "How did you reach our incomparable palace? Not many strangers find their way here."

"We came . . ." said Toby.

"It is fortunate that I was just taking my daily walk round the exquisite gardens when you arrived," went on the Interpreter. "Did you wish to have an audience with the Exceedingly

Honourable Emperor? I regret that he is in bed with a heavy cold, and cannot see anyone at present. The Extremely Honourable Empress and the Highly Honourable Lord Chamberlain are looking after him."

"I'm sorry to hear that," said Toby. "You see . . ."

"A most unfortunate incident. Some clever fellow tried to trick him into buying an invisible suit of clothes, and the Exceedingly Honourable Emperor went parading round the grounds with, pardon me, absolutely nothing on! And in front of all the Slightly Honourable Cleaners and the Not Very Honourable Dishwashers, too. Well, it's no wonder he caught a cold."

"Yes, of course," said Toby. "Well, what we are here for . . ."

"At any rate, the Highly Dishourable Con-man was suitably punished. He was sent into exile to the snow-bound plains of Outer Freezia, wearing nothing but his own invisible clothes. That'll larn him!"

Toby made another attempt to get a word in. "We have come because we have heard that the Emperor . . ."

"Ah, yes, of course! You have heard that the Exceedingly Honourable Emperor is one of the wisest men in the world, and you wish to consult him on a Matter of Importance. But did you realize that whole poems have been written about his wisdom, and not just by himself! I am sure you would like to hear one of them."

Toby was getting very fidgety because the time was going on and they seemed to be getting nowhere, but the Interpreter continued without waiting for a reply,

> "The Emperor of Nos Mo King
> Knows very nearly everything –
> He knows the 'where' and 'what' and 'why'
> Of birds that swim and fish that fly,
>
> Why gliders glide and spiders spin,
> Why seals are fat and eels are thin,
> Why bears are big and hares are small,
> Why shrubs are short and trees are tall,
>
> Why mice are nice and lice are not,
> Why ice is cold and spice is hot,
> Why flies can fly and fleas can tease,
> Why stoats have coats and goats give cheese,
>
> He knows what makes the glowworms glow,
> Why quails are quick and snails are slow,
> But even he knows not, I'm told,
> The way to cure the common cold.

"Which is a pity in the present circumstances," he concluded. "However, he is certainly as wise as the legendary Sage Who Knew His Onions, who lived in the time of the Emperor Yu Can Chu. But we digress. You were saying . . .?"

"I was *trying* to say that this is a very clever invention we have brought for the Emperor," said Toby, pointing to the Walkie-Talkie."

"Ah, yes, the Mobile Scarecrow," said the Interpreter. "Most useful for the vegetable garden. I shall present it to His Exceeding Highness as soon as he has recovered from his cold."

However, by this time Dee Lee was nearly exploding with impatience. They had been half an hour already, and not a word said about Dah Lee. Now she flapped up and down in front of the Interpreter, and quacked loudly,

"And we have brought it in exchange for my husband, Dah Lee, who is being held prisoner in the palace."

Suddenly there was dead silence. For a few moments the Interpreter was so furious he could not utter a word. At last he managed to splutter,

"No, you don't understand," said Toby.

"WHAT!" thundered the Interpreter, drawing himself up to his full five foot two inches. "You dare to suggest that I, the Relatively Honourable Interpreter, DO NOT UNDERSTAND! This is

an insult worthy of thirty days in an Extremely Uncomfortable Dungeon"

"Oh dear!" said Toby. He got up and switched on the little robot, which at once trotted off and said to the nearest bush, "Pleased-to-meet-you-is-there-any-news-have-you-heard-any-good-gossip-recently?"

"It's a Walkie-Talkie," explained Toby. "It walks the dog and talks to the neighbours, and tells you all they said when it comes back." A smile spread over the Interpreter's face. *At last we are getting somewhere*, thought Toby.

"*In exchange*, did you say? You bring a free and generous gift, and expect the Exceedingly Honourable Emperor to give you something in *exchange*! But this is a crime punishable by being hung by your toes over a very large cooking pot, and basted with boiling oil until you Miserably Expire! I am not sure what the punishment is for ducks, but we will soon find out!"

He called out something in Nosmokinian, and two large, uniformed guards appeared at once from the shrubbery behind them.

"Bleng blimpa slipwik norraglimp shrabbilups!" ordered the Interpreter. Then he strode off in the direction of the palace. One of the guards grabbed Dee Lee, and tucked her firmly under his arm, where she squawked furiously. The other one picked up the conspicuous tangerine chameleon, who was trying to hide under the bench.

"Well, now we are in the soup," said Toby, as they waited miserably for the Interpreter's return.

"Don't talk about soup," said Dee Lee. "It makes me very nervous."

"Pleased-to-meet-you-is-there-any-news-have-you-heard-any-good-gossip-recently?" said the Walkie-Talkie, who had just bumped into one of the guards.

"Aw, shut up!" said Toby, switching it off.

Before long the Relatively Honourable Interpreter came back, saying,

"I have consulted the Right Honourable Prime Minister. She agrees with me that the chief offender in this case is the Dishonourable Duck." Ignoring Dee Lee's indignant quack, he went on, "She will therefore be boiled in oil one week from today, unless she can justify her existence by learning to sing like a nightingale within that time. We fear that the Exceedingly Honourable Emperor's illness may be partly due to pining for the aforementioned bird. Her accomplices will be ceremoniously kicked out of the grounds, and if you ever set foot in here again, the cauldron is waiting. By the way, thank you for the present."

He called out something in Nosmokinian to the gatekeeper, then said, "Come!" to the Walkie-Talkie. When it took no notice, he started half-carrying, half dragging it towards the palace, followed by the guard still carrying Dee Lee. In spite of all Toby's and Hardly Visible's protests, they found themselves being pushed out of the gate by the other guard, with some willing help from the Averagely Honourable Gatekeeper's boot. They landed outside in the dust, and the great gate clanged shut behind them.

Chapter 11 ~ Just in Case . . .

It took Toby a few moments to get his breath back, then he realized that he was wasting still more time, and set off running back to the Toothsayer's house as fast as his legs would carry him.

"Here, wait for me!" said a tangerine squeak behind him, and he stopped to let the chameleon scramble up into his pocket again. Hardly Visible was a good sprinter, but he preferred to get a lift for any journey longer than two or three minutes.

"Oh, excruciating extractions!" said the Toothsayer when they had gasped out their story. "I should have known their High-and-Mightinesses at the palace would not see reason. But there is no more you can do now. You must get to the Prism Tree before Slubblejum, or the whole world will be coming to a sticky end, not just a pair of ducks."

"But . . ." said Toby.

"No buts!" said the Toothsayer. "That's hard facts, and you just have to bite the bullet, as they say. Besides, we are not far from a moonless night, and if you miss that, you will have to wait a whole month for the next one. You cannot take even a small cutting except when there is no moon, remember. Have you a good, sharp penknife? Good . . . Now put this on – you will be glad of it later." She produced a padded jacket with a hood. It was a bit big for Toby, but with the cuffs turned back it made quite a good full-length coat.

"I've packed a rucksack for you," she added, and helped him to settle it on his back. "Now, there are only two ways to get to the Prism Tree. You can fly on the back of a dragon, but alas! – where are the dragons when you need them?"

"I think we have had enough of dragons," said Toby.

"Otherwise you have to go on foot through the Oki Koki pass that runs beside Mount Nevarest. Nevarest is the twin of Evarest, of course. The experts have never decided which is the higher, because there is a bit of a problem about measuring the last few feet. The Oki Koki river begins its life as a glacier up there, then gradually turns into the main river of Nos Mo King. I've put a map in your rucksack. Off you go, then – *Up the airy mountain, down the rushy glen . . .*" She gave a

sudden toothless grin. "But you had better take some Flee Powder with you. Just in case."

"Beg your pardon!" said Toby.

"Flee Powder," she repeated, and produced an old-fashioned spray gun, like the kind used to spray pests in the garden. "It's my very latest invention. If you spray it on anything, it will flee away at once, though to tell the tooth, I don't know where it goes. So do be careful about getting it on your toes. GET DOWN SHEP!" The Small Hairy Earth Pig was trying to poke his nose into the rucksack.

"Just lookin'" grunted the pig, startling Toby, who had not realized it could speak English.

"And as for the ducks," added the Toothsayer. "I'll think of something to help them. Spiders' incisors! I may have to learn to sing like a night-ingale myself!" She let out a loud cackle at this, while Shep gave a scornful snort.

Toby grasped the Flee Powder, and Hardly Visible decided to settle himself comfortably in the hood of the jacket, and they were ready for their trek across the roof of the world.

"Now, hurry, hurry!" said the Toothsayer. "Remember there is no time to lose." She heaved a great sigh, and added,

> *"What is this life if, full of care,*
> *We have no time to comb our hair?"*

As they went down the hill, they could hear her voice fading into the distance behind them:

> *"What is this life if, full of woes,*
> *We have no time to blow our nose?*
>
> *What is this life if, full of hope,*
> *We slip upon a bar of soap?*
>
> *What is this life if, full of whisky,*
> *We've only time for feeling frisky . . ."*

Chapter 12 ~ Whoosh!

As soon as Toby got to the bottom of the Tooth-sayer's hill he stopped and opened the rucksack. Although he realized the need to hurry, it was now mid-afternoon and he had only had one jelly baby since breakfast on the *Catty Sark*. He found that, besides the map, the rucksack contained several tins of baked beans, a tin opener, a flask of water and an incredible quantity of sweets of all kinds, done up neatly in little paper bags.

"Oh, great!" he said to Hardly Visible. "Cold beans are my favourite. And they say sweets give you energy – just the thing for climbing the Himalayas."

He felt much better after his meal, and decided the best way to travel was to use scouts' pace – running twenty paces, then walking twenty paces. He kept this up for a couple of hours, away from the town and towards the distant mountains, had

another short break, then pressed on again as fast as he could. Somehow the white-capped mountains never seemed to get any nearer. They saw no sign of humans, and only a few animals. Once they met a goat, who stopped and stared at them. Hardly Visible greeted it with,

> *"A goat in the French Pyrenees*
> *Used to jump up as high as the trees;*
> *He said, when asked why,*
> *'I'm not trying to fly,*
> *But I can't get away from these fleas!'"*

"Bah!" said the goat, and skipped away up the hillside.

"Well, it wouldn't rhyme with Himalayas," said Hardly apologetically.

"I wish I could leap up the hills like he does," said Toby. By now it was almost dark, but they struggled on for another hour or so until they reached a small grove of trees near a stream, where they had their supper.

"Good job I like cold beans," said Toby. He had decided to keep the sweets for when he really needed energy on the journey. As he curled up in a little hollow for the night, he was about to set his alarm watch for the morning, but discovered it was missing.

"Drat!" he said. "I knew I should have got that strap fixed." The next morning, however, he was awake well before dawn, in spite of his tiredness. He knew there was something dreadful hanging over him, and for a moment he couldn't think what it was. Then he remembered that living things would never see the sun rise again if he didn't reach the Prism Tree in time.

After a quick bean breakfast, they set off for a day's journey that was very much like the previous one, except that the hills became steeper each time they had to climb one. The terrain was definitely becoming mountainous, and not just hilly. Also, it was growing steadily colder, and Toby at last began to be glad of the padded coat.

"We'll just have to stop for lunch," he said at last. "I can't go another step. Ah, well – beans are better than nothing, I suppose." He unslung the rucksack, opened a tin for himself, and took out the Toothsayer's map once more. In the distance they could now see quite clearly the outline of Mount Nevarest on their left, and Mount Proppacoppakettle on their right. The Toothsayer had told them that the bit that stuck out like a spout, and gave Proppacoppakettle its name, was one of the most difficult climbs in the world. Hence the expression "up the spout" if you were in difficulties.

Toby and Hardly Visible were so busy admiring the view that they did not notice something creeping up behind them. Several somethings, in fact. Somethings with cat-like features, and brightly coloured scales on their backs. Nethercats!

"Now we've got you!" said Slubblejum.

"No, you haven't!" said Toby, jumping to his feet and backing away. "Anyway, how did *you* get here?"

"A little bird told us the way – or a little pig, rather."

"The Toothsayer's pig, I suppose," said Toby gloomily.

"That's right," said Slubblejum. "He didn't take much persuading to tell us all he knew, did he, my hearties?" The "hearties" sniggered. "Just a short conversation about bacon sandwiches, and he would do anything for us – isn't that right? Now, we'll have that map, if you don't mind." He made a sudden pounce and picked it up before Toby could stop him.

"You've got it all wrong," said Toby. "The Toothsayer told us that if you cut down the Prism Tree, everything in the world will die."

"Rubbish!" said Slubblejum.

"It's true!" protested Toby. "Everything depends on chlory . . . that green stuff, and if you turn it grey the plants will die, then the animals and everything. Even nethercats."

"Nuts!" said Slubblejum cheerfully. "That old witch just told you that because she doesn't want to spoil the nice view from her window. But fine feathers butter no parsnips with me. Have a look at this map, Weedy. That thing like a triangular lollipop must be the famous Prism Tree . . ."

Finkleweed and the other nethercats crowded round him, all trying to see the map at once. Slubblejum looked up at Toby and started jeering, "Yah, silly little yuman! You can't do anything to stop us now!"

Oh, can't I! thought Toby, but he didn't say it out loud. He quietly took the spray gun of Flee Powder from his rucksack, and squeezed it as hard as he could over the whole bunch of nethercats.

Whoosh! went Slubblejum.

Whoosh! went Finkelweed.

Whoosh! went the rest of the nethercats, complete with the saws and axes they were carrying. Suddenly Toby and Hardly Visible were alone once more, with nothing to show that they had had any visitors.

"Phew!" squeaked the chameleon, as he emerged from behind a rock where he had been hiding. "That stuff really works, doesn't it?"

"It sure does," said Toby. "The only problem is, they have got our map, but what could I do?"

"Never mind maps," said Hardly. "Even you must know it by heart by now, and the compass in my chest is getting stronger all the time."

They set off again, both of them feeling so cheerful at having got rid of the nethercats so easily that they nearly danced down the hillside. Their way now led into the broad valley where they could see the Oki Koki like a great, sparkling snake in the distance. After they had crossed that valley, it would be uphill all the way, but at least they would be able to push on steadily, without being bothered by nethercats.

"I hope the Flee Powder has blown them all the way to Australia," said Toby. "Come on, let's see if we can reach the river by nightfall."

Hardly Visible did not answer, because he was too busy watching a lone eagle flying overhead. He was not at all keen on large birds, and hid under a nearby rock until it had gone. When he had recovered from his fright, he emerged and said,

> "A certain bald eagle called Billy
> Found the fresh mountain air rather chilly,
> So he purchased a few
> Ostrich feathers and glue,
> And made himself warm, white and frilly."

Chapter 13 ~ Unexpected Meeting

"Oh dear," said Toby as they stopped beside the river bank, "I do wish I liked cold beans!" When he opened the rucksack, however, he found he was down to the very last tin. Nothing but sweets from now on. After supper they found a suitable place for the night, sheltered among a clump of trees. Toby had blisters, and was beginning to feel discouraged again.

"The Toothsayer said the Himalayas were crawling with tourists these days," he said. "I do wish we would meet some who could help us. It has been fairly easy so far, but I don't know how we are going to tackle the Eeeeeeee!"

The last remark was because something had just jumped out from behind a tree and grabbed him. He was pulled to his feet and found himself looking into the grinning, coppery face of the nethercat bosun, Fattascratch. At the same time he could see the plump, purple cook holding up the squirming Hardly Visible by his tail. Little yellow Scaredy-cat was looking on nervously as if he didn't know what to do with himself.

"So we meet again," said Fattascratch. "What a hunexpected pleasure!" Toby's first reaction was to try to pull the spray gun out of his rucksack. Unfortunately, Fattascratch was a lot quicker than Slubblejum had been, and grabbed it off him. He held it out of Toby's reach, and painfully read the label, "F-l-e-e- P-o-w-d-e-r."

"What's this, then?" he demanded. "To get the fleas off your little friend, is it? "Old 'im up, Bogglewick – let's smother the little 'orror."

The plump nethercat held up the chameleon at arm's length, but Toby called out "NO!" so loudly that Fattascratch stopped in his tracks.

"What's the matter?" he asked. "What is it, dynamite?"

Young Scaredy-cat had by now come close enough to read the label, "It's s-sp-spelt funny," he said. "It must be p-powder to make things flee, not, p-p-p-powder for f-f-fleas."

"Who asked you?" snapped Fattascratch, then he turned back to Toby.

"I can see it's for making things flee," he said, "But where does they get to, that's the question?"

"I don't know," said Toby. "Nobody knows."

"'Ow very hinteresting," said Fattascratch, pointing the spray gun at Toby. "You may find out before you're much older." Then he turned to Hardly Visible, and gave the squirming chameleon a poke with his claw.

"This must be my lucky day," he said with a grin. "You can lead us to that there Prism Tree before Cap'n Slubblejum finds it. It's time 'e learned 'e's not the cleverest nethercat in the world. I can just see 'is face when 'e finds we've got there first. Now, hif you don't co-hoperate and show us the way, I will blow your yuman friend into Never Never Land, and you will be left with us all by your little self, got it? So just be a good little kermealyron and do as you're told . . . or else."

Hardly Visible nodded violently, as well as he could upside-down, and Fattascratch turned back to Toby.

"Come on, you – pick up your bag and get moving. We'll pack some provisions and set off at dawn tomorrow."

Toby picked up the rucksack, but also started trying to explain about the Prism Tree. Fattascratch gave him a resounding swipe with his webbed paw that made Toby's head sing.

"Shut up!" he said. "Cabin boys are seen and not 'eard while I'm around. It's time we 'ad some discipline on this ship, if you hask me."

What ship? thought Toby, but he soon found out. As they came round a bend in the river, he saw the *Catty Sark*, firmly grounded on a group of rocks in mid-stream. Her figurehead scowled as fiercely as ever, but the rest of the ship was a sorry sight. She was listing over at a drunken angle, and her sails were not furled properly, but simply drooping from the masts in the still, cold air. Evidently Fattascratch had got bored with minding the ship downstream, and had sailed up the river just a little bit too far.

"If our clever Cap'n 'adn't gone off with all the tools, we could 'ave mended that by now," said Fattascratch. "That", of course, was the gaping hole in the ship's side.

As soon as they had scrambled over the rocks onto the ship, Fattascratch roared at the young yellow nethercat to fetch a seive "at the double".

"A w-w-what?" stuttered Scaredy-cat.

"A seive!" shouted Fattascratch. 'S-I-V-E. You deaf, or something? And fetch some string while you are at it."

"Y-yes, Sir," said Scaredy-cat, and ran off to the galley. By the time he came back, Fattascratch had found an old piece of plank in a corner of the deck.

"Bring that kermealyron 'ere," he ordered the purple one. Hardly Visible trembled, convinced that this was going to be the small torture chamber he had been threatened with earlier, while Toby felt helpless with the spray gun still pointing at him. All that happened, however, was that the chameleon was put on the piece of wood, then the seive was tied firmly over his head with the string. It formed a very effective little cage.

"Take 'em below decks!" ordered Fattascratch. "And tie up the yuman."

A few minutes later, Toby found himself tied up in a corner of the hold, with the chameleon's cage beside him.

"Are you okay, Hardly?" he asked.

"Could be worse," squeaked the chameleon. "But no room to swing a cat, as you might say."

"Do you have to be so blooming cheerful!" said Toby. He was nearly in despair at the turn of events. He felt that they might have had a chance to talk Slubblejum out of his scheme, if he would listen long enough, but Fattascratch was just the type to go ahead and cut down the Prism Tree out of spite, even if he did know it would mean the end of the world. They had really landed out of the frying pan into the fire this time.

Chapter 14 ~ Himalayan Hustle

Toby would always remember the following day as the day of the hustle. After being hustled onto the deck before dawn, he was allowed about two minutes to eat a bowl of lumpy porridge (Fattascratch had been hustling the cook as well). Then he was hustled into filling up his rucksack with some of the mouldy old ship's biscuits. Fattascratch never stopped to notice that it was two thirds full of sweets already. Then he was hustled off the ship and along the river bank. The bosun had shaken out of Hardly Visible the information that they should follow the river towards the mountains, and that was all he needed to know for now.

Little Scaredy-cat was sent to the front, followed by the podgy Bogglewick. They both had sacks of provisions over their shoulders, but Scaredy-cat's was the heavier. He could hardly stagger under it. Then came Toby with his rucksack, and finally Fattascratch, carrying the chameleon still tied up in the seive, and brandishing the Flee Powder. He also had a coil of rope round his shoulders, and a small, rusty saw the other nethercats had not bothered to take.

Every few minutes the big, ginger Fattascratch would shout "'Urry up there!" or "What are you dawdling for?" It was mainly Scaredy-cat he was shouting at, but it was Toby who got the poke in the back that went with his words. They had set out before sunrise, with a frost on the ground and a clammy mist in the air. Even when the sun did come out, it seemed unable to make any impression on the cold air, and by the time they had been going for a couple of hours it was starting to snow. Toby was glad that his jacket had a hood, and long cuffs which he could turn down to keep his hands fairly warm. The nethercats did not seem to feel the cold, but the unfortunate Hardly Visible got the worst of it. He curled up into a tight ball inside his seive cage and tried, unsuccessfully, to go to sleep.

Lunch time was a fiasco. Apparently the sacks carried by Scaredy-cat and Bogglewick were almost entirely filled with oatmeal and dried milk to make porridge, and Scaredy-cat was also supposed to be carrying a small primus stove and the matches. But when he opened his sack there were no matches.

There followed a lot of shouting, with Fattascratch blaming Bogglewick, and Bogglewick blaming Fattascratch, and everybody blaming Scaredy-cat (whose real name turned out to be Limbledrip). When the unfortunate Scaredy-cat began to stutter an excuse, Fattascratch picked up the primus stove and threw it at him, hitting him painfully on the shoulder. Then he grabbed Toby's rucksack, having apparently forgotten what was in it.

"What you got there?" he asked. Then, seeing the mouldy ship's biscuits on the top, he said, "Yuk! Only good enough for yumans!" He ordered Bogglewick and Scaredy-cat to go fishing in the river, which already had big lumps of ice floating in it. They eventually managed to catch enough fish to satisfy the three nethercats, but not without Fattascratch working himself into an even worse temper because of the delay.

At this stage of the proceedings, a loud squeak came from the improvised cage which was lying on the ground:

> *"There's something quite subtle and inner*
> *That tells me it's time for my dinner,*
> *And the longer I wait*
> *Without food on my plate,*
> *The more I get thinner and thinner."*

"Give him some biscuits, you!" Fattascratch said to Toby. "Anything to stop him whining."

"He's going to freeze to death if you don't let him out of that cage," said Toby. "He usually rides in my pocket." To his surprise, Fattascratch agreed to let the chameleon out, partly because he was fed up with carrying the piece of plank with the cage, and also because he was afraid if anything happened to Hardly they would never find the

Prism Tree. So when they set off again, Hardly Visible was once more curled up in Toby's pocket, but with his back leg tied to the strap of the rucksack with a piece of string, just in case he should try any tricks.

After that, the rest of the day was even more of a hustle. They left the sacks of oatmeal behind so as to travel faster. The ground was difficult to walk over, as for much of the time it consisted of loose, shaly stones with a thin covering of snow. Toby felt he was turning into a walking machine as he went on putting one foot in front of the other, with his head down against the snow.

However, all bad things, like all good things, come to an end. At last, just as it was beginning to get dark, Fattascratch spotted a small cave, and decided it was time to stop for the night. He yawned and stretched, then gave a great purr of satisfaction.

"I reckon that's a good day's march," he said. "'Ow much farther to the Prism Tree, eh, ker-mealyron?" He gave Hardly Visible a shake.

"Don't know," squeaked the chameleon.

"Leave him!" said Toby. "And if you cut down the tree you'll destroy . . ." He was cut short by a swipe from an angry paw.

"Be quiet or I'll tie you up and dump you in the river," said Fattascratch. "You're no use to us anyway." Then he sent the other two nethercats to do some fishing in the freezing water, while he made himself comfortable in the cave. Even they were shivering by the time they came back with a few small fish. Toby and Hardly Visible were allowed biscuits and water, before being tied up for the night.

Toby tossed and turned for a long time before getting off to sleep on the rocky floor. No matter how hard he tried, he couldn't think of any way out of their dreadful situation. But somehow, *somehow*, they must try to escape and get to the Prism Tree before Fattascratch.

When he at last got to sleep, he dreamed that he was still being hustled through the snow, faster and faster and faster, until he found that Fattascratch was chasing him round a tree with a big axe. He woke with a start to find that he was being shaken by a real nethercat.

15 ~ Plonk

Toby stared stupidly at Scaredy-cat. "Is it morning already?" Then he realized that the cave was empty. "Where are the others?" he asked.

"They've gone," said Scaredy-cat, who was busy untying the rope around Toby's wrists.

"What do you mean, gone?" asked Toby, sitting up with a jerk. The small, yellow nethercat gave a grin. It was the first time Toby had ever seen him look cheerful.

"I sprayed them with your Flee Powder while they were asleep," he said. "At last I've got my own back on that bullying bosun!"

Toby sprang to his feet with a shout of "Whoopee!" and tripped over the rope round his ankles, which was only half undone. "That's the best thing you've done for a long time," he said as he disentangled himself. "Now you can come with us to rescue the Prism Tree."

But the pale little nethercat was already on his way out of the cave and running towards the river.

"No fear!" he called over his shoulder. "I don't care if the world is grey or sky-blue pink. All I want is to find a warmer bit of the river and settle down."

"Stop! Scaredy . . . Limbledrip!" shouted Toby, as he chased after the bounding nethercat. "You don't realize. If the tree is cut down . . ."

It was no use. He was just in time to see Scaredy-cat slip into the icy stream, and swim off down the river as fast as only a nethercat can.

"Brrrr!" said Toby, as he watched him go. "I'm glad I don't live in a cold river, anyway."

He went back to release Hardly Visible, who was jumping up and down with excitement, in spite of the string tied round his legs. The chameleon had, of course, heard what had happened.

"Did you notice that Scaredy-cat never stuttered once?" remarked Toby. "It must have been just fear of old Scratchy that was making him do it."

Hardly Visible replied,

"There once was a cow in Calcutta,
Who mooed with a terrible stutter,
Every m-m-m-moo
Made her shake through and through,
And the milk came out b-b-b-butter."

Then, as soon as his feet were untied, he did a rapid scamper round and round the cave to get warmed up, while Toby picked up his rucksack and the container of Flee Powder, which Scaredy-cat had left lying on the ground.

They had a quick breakfast of biscuits and freezing cold water from the river, where Toby also filled his flask, in case it should be completely frozen over next time they wanted a drink. He did not touch the sweets, because he thought they would keep better than the old biscuits.

"Do come on, Hardly!" he called to the chameleon, who was still scuttling around because he was so pleased at being free again. "We are in a hurry, don't forget – whether old Scratchy is there to chase us or not. We don't really know where all those nethercats have got to – we just know that there are two lots of them looking for the Prism Tree. We simply have to get there first, whatever happens."

So for the next three hours or so, Toby drove himself forward as hard as if Fattascratch were still behind him. It was snowing just enough to make the rocky ground slippery, and the snow blew into his eyes continually, making progress very difficult. Then he simply had to stop for lunch and a rest.

"Cheer me up, Hardly," he said. "I could do with a nice, jolly poem right now."

"I'm cold!" complained the chameleon. "I don't feel very jolly. And say what you like, biscuit crumbs are not a patch on earwigs. Anyway, what do you want a poem about?"

"Not a notion," said Toby. Hardly Visible thought for a minute, than recited,

> *"'Twas on a dark and gloomy night,*
> *The fog was all around,*
> *A muffled shape came into sight,*
> *A-bumping on the ground;*
> *A fearful voice resounded,*
> *It would make your blood to freeze –*
> *'It's the Nottagottanotion*
> *With the knobulated knees!'*

Oh, he lives on leeks and custard
And he's worse than all your fears –
He's the Nottagottanotion
With elasticated ears.

Oh, how could I describe the dreadful
'Notion standing there?
His eyes, his nose, his ankle-socks,
The tangles in his hair!
The sound to strike with terror
Of the horrorific sneeze
Of the Nottagottanotion
With the knobulated knees!

Oh, he lives on tea and mustard
And he's worse than all your fears –
He puts mustard in his custard
And he stirs it with his ears!

He is very fond of artichokes
And puts them in a stew,
With girls and boys and mustard
And a pinch of pepper too;
So let's all say, 'Hip hip hooray!'
And give three hearty cheers
For the Nottagottanotion
With elasticated ears . . .

For the Nottagottanotion
Who is everything you please,
With the corrugated elbows
And the knobulated knees!"

"Well, I hope we don't meet *him*," said Toby as they set off again through the snow, which was coming on more heavily now. "And this stupid snow doesn't help." He gave a kick to a large mound of it that lay in his path. The mound made a noise like the baa-ing of an overgrown sheep, then got up and ran away, leaving a trail of enormous footprints behind it.

For a moment, Toby stood literally shaking in his shoes.

"Hardly," he whispered, then he felt silly whispering in the middle of nowhere, and forced himself to speak out loud. "Hardly, do you realize what that was?"

"A whitewashed gorilla?" said a muffled voice from somewhere under the snow.

"I think it must have been a yeti," said Toby.

"A whatti?" asked the chameleon, his small, tangerine head popping out again.

"A yeti. You know, the Abominable Snowman."

"A-b-b-bominable . . ."

"That's what they call it," said Toby. "There are lots of reports of it being seen by climbers, but somehow no one ever gets a decent photograph. I don't suppose we'll ever lay eyes on it again."

He couldn't have been more wrong. There was only one thing in the world stronger than the yeti's desire to remain hidden, and that was his love of sweets. He could smell Toby's rucksack half a mile away, and it drew him like a magnet. So, as Toby and the chameleon set off once more, a large, white, shambling figure gradually crept up behind them . . .

Toby stopped dead. Something was breathing very heavily down his neck. Very slowly, he turned his head and looked behind him. The big, shaggy monster was just stretching out a paw towards the rucksack. Toby gave a yell, and the startled yeti ran off for a few yards, but the smell of the rucksack was too much for him. He stopped and looked at Toby with his head on one side, and held out a great paw.

"Sweeties?" he said.

"So that's what you want," said Toby. "Well, I haven't any to spare. They have to last until I get across the Himalayas."

The yeti gave a whimper, and looked so disappointed that Toby gave in. "Oh, all right," he said. "Just two and no more." He fished out two boiled sweets, and threw them to the yeti, who put them in his mouth, paper and all, and crunched loudly.

"More," he said hopefully.

"No more," said Toby.

"More, more!" said the yeti, stamping his great foot.

"No more," said Toby.

The yeti seemed to be thinking hard. After a few moments, he gave Toby a grimace that was meant to be a smile, and said, "You give sweeties, me take peoples." He attempted to pat himself on the back, then pointed at the mountain pass ahead.

"What do you think, Hardly?" asked Toby. "He seems harmless enough."

"You expect me to ride on that overgrown hearth-rug?" squeaked the chameleon.

"Best offer you'll get this year," said Toby, who was very much aware of his blisters. "And ten times quicker than going on foot. Okay, yeti, it's a deal."

"Plonk," said the yeti.

"Pardon?"

"Plonk!" repeated the yeti, giving himself a thump on the chest.

"Oh, I see, that's your name. Well, I'm Toby, and you can have half the sweets now, and the rest when we get to the other side of Mount Nevarest, where the Prism Tree grows. Understand?"

The yeti grimaced again, and made a grab for the rucksack. Toby just managed to save it from him, and handed out about half the small bags of sweets, hastily closing the rucksack again while the yeti was eating them, a whole bag at a time. Then he climbed up onto the yeti's back, and found that the best position was right up on his shoulders, holding onto the woolly hair on top of his head. The chameleon followed rather reluctantly.

"Off we go, Plonk," said Toby. "I don't know what we would have done without you."

Chapter 16 ~ On Top of the World

The yeti's speed was so great that they completed in one day a journey that would otherwise have taken Toby a whole week. For a while they followed the course of the Oki Koki, now a wide glacier, then the yeti started climbing up an almost vertical, icy slope. Although his hands and feet were so big, he seemed able to hold on by the smallest of fingerholds. After a while, Toby looked down, then wished he hadn't. There were actually clouds beneath them, and he daren't think what might be below that.

"Er, Plonk," he said. "Are you sure you know the way? We have to get to the Prism Tree valley, you know."

'Plonk know Prism Tree," came the reply. "Very pretty. Plonk like."

"Oh, well," said Toby. "You know best."

"Pass go round about," explained the yeti.

Toby was not so sure about that, but he hadn't much choice at this stage. He just closed his eyes and clung on tight. At last, after what seemed like hours of climbing, he heard the yeti's voice again.

"We reach top of world. You watch pretty sunset."

Toby was glad to slip down from the yeti's back and stretch his legs even for a few minutes. The thin mountain air was hard to breathe, but what really took his breath away was the view. The sun was just setting, and its reflected light turned the snowy tops of the surrounding mountains a wonderful glowing orange colour, which faded into deep pink as they watched, and then turned to a purplish grey as night fell. All the colours were echoed in the clouds, which stretched beneath them like a solid carpet of cotton wool.

"Much slow. Plonk go over top. Pretty view from Mount Nevarest. You like."

"I think I'll be an artist after all," said Toby, half to himself. "It would be worth crossing the Himalayas just to save the colours." The thought reminded him of Slubblejum and Fattascratch. He simply had to get to the Prism Tree before them, or there would not only be no colours in the future, but no people to see them – no birds, no animals, just lifeless grey mountains for ever more.

"Come on, Plonk," he said to the yeti, who was sitting with his chin on his great, hairy paws. "We must keep moving. We can't stay here for the night, can we?"

"We go down quick, quick," said the yeti. "You see!"

Toby looked at the precipice below them and gulped, but there was nothing for it but to climb onto the yeti's shoulders again, and hold on very tight. The chameleon had not bothered to get down, and was still buried in the long fur at the back of Plonk's head. The yeti set off down the other side of Nevarest at breakneck speed.

Toby lost all sense of time, but it could only have been about half an hour later that the yeti stopped again. There was still some light in the sky, and when Toby dared to open his eyes, he saw that they had stopped under an overhanging part of the cliff face that would give them some shelter.

"Good place for night," said the yeti. "We camp now."

Toby had his usual meal of ship's biscuits, and the yeti was allowed just one handful of sweets – one of Toby's handfuls, that is, not his own.

"Would you like some biscuit crumbs, Hardly?" asked Toby. "Sorry there is nothing else for you."

The chameleon stuck his head out from the yeti's fur, licked his tangerine lips and said, "You'd be surprised!"

"Ugh!" said Toby. All of a sudden he felt rather itchy.

As they settled down for the night, the yeti made a good windbreak as well as a safety barrier for the others. There was no danger of them rolling off the ledge of rock with his great bulk there to stop them.

They were now below the clouds again, but through a gap in them Toby caught a glimpse of a dainty sliver of a moon, curving to the left.

> *"Moon on the right is getting bright,*
> *Moon on the left is all that's left,"*

he murmured to himself. "That means tomorrow will be a moonless night, so we must reach the Prism . . . Tr . . ." Then he fell asleep.

Chapter 17 ~ The Prism Tree

The next day dawned bright and clear, although it was still bitterly cold. They set off again without any breakfast, because Toby was afraid if he opened the rucksack at all, the yeti might grab the rest of the sweets and run off. However, Plonk was very well behaved, and seemed as eager as Toby to get to their journey's end. He went half-scrambling, half-sliding down the mountainside as if Mount Nevarest were just a great big helter-skelter at a fairground. After what seemed like a couple of hours of this, he stopped abruptly and said,

"We come. I go now."

Toby slid down, feeling very relieved to have solid ground under his feet again. He found himself looking out from a steep outcrop of rock. Spread in front of them lay a great valley, several miles across. Its slopes were lined with trees of many different kinds, but it was impossible to see what lay in the middle of it, because the air was filled with a kind of shimmering light, like a heat haze. They could see a rough, but fairly easy path leading down from their viewpoint towards the valley floor.

"Prism Tree Valley!" announced the yeti, as proudly as if he had made it himself for the occasion.

"At last!" said Toby. "Well, here are the rest of your sweets. I must say, you have earned them. Here, why don't you keep the rucksack as well? It's no use to me now." He handed over the rucksack with the rest of the sweets.

Plonk was delighted with this extra reward, and tried to shake Toby's hand. The result was more like shaking Toby, and the boy was glad when it stopped. The yeti filled his mouth with sweets, hung the rucksack over his wrist like a handbag, and chased off up the mountainside again.

"He never seems to get tired, that fellow," said Toby as he and Hardly Visible made their way carefully down the uneven path. Although it was no longer a sheer mountainside, it was still quite steep at first, leading them through pines and fir trees. Then the slope gradually evened out, and they found themselves surrounded by more different kinds of trees than they had ever dreamed of.

Some Toby knew the names of – poplars and birches, oaks and chestnuts, holly bushes and hawthorns. Many more he had never seen before – some tall and graceful, some thick and sturdy, some short and spiky. Then came blossom trees of all kinds – pink and white, red and yellow, orange and lilac. Among them, fruit trees were producing apples and pears, plums and cherries, nuts and berries of all kinds.

"The seasons seem to be all mixed up together in this place," said Toby to Hardly Visible. However, the chameleon was much more interested in that fact that each kind of tree seemed to have its own form of insect life. He had never discovered so many delicious new tastes in such a short space of time. He dashed around from one tree to another, while Toby ate some fruit, and stopped to quench his thirst at a splashing mountain stream. It was much warmer now, and he was glad to take off the padded jacket and leave it hanging over a bush, just taking the Flee Powder with him.

There were lots of small, brightly-coloured birds around, filling the air with their cheerful songs, and there was another sound in the background as well – a kind of musical tinkling, but Toby couldn't make out what it was. It gradually grew louder as they approached the middle of the valley.

At last the dappled light and shade of the trees
gave way to a brighter light, and they found
themselves out in full sunshine again. A great
clearing lay before them. The grass beneath their
feet was short and firm, and dotted with tiny
flowers.

In the middle of the clearing was something
that, if it had been perfectly still, would have
looked like a great fountain of ice. It sprang out
of the ground to a tremendous height, then curved
over on every side in a beautiful, graceful move-

ment. Its shape was like a gigantic weeping willow, but the lower branches did not cascade right down to the ground, but remained suspended in mid air so high that an ordinary oak or beech tree could have grown beneath them.

As Toby and the chameleon walked slowly towards the tree, they could see that it was made up of millions of tiny leaves, like icicles. It moved constantly in the gentle breeze that blew around it, and its leaves sparkled and shimmered with little flashes of light of every colour at once. As they did so, they tinkled like tiny glass bells, filling the air with the mysterious chiming sound Toby had heard earlier.

Around the tree's broad trunk, the flowers in the grass fell into a pattern of rings. The biggest, outer ring was of violets; inside that was a ring of very dark blue flowers, then one of light blue, one of green (not just grass, but some kind of bright green flowers), then yellow, orange, and the smallest ring next to the tree of bright red campions.

Toby felt he would like to stay there for ever just to watch the tree and listen to its silvery music. He looked down at Hardly Visible, who was near his feet, and saw that something very strange was happening to the chameleon. It was as if ripples of colour were running along his body from head to tail, echoing the rings of flowers –

red, orange, yellow, green, blue, indigo and violet. Then, suddenly, the chameleon disappeared.

"Hardly, where are you?" gasped Toby.

"Here, of course, where do you think?" said the familiar squeak. Then Toby saw the outline of the chameleon's shape, and realized that he was now blending in with the grass, and that his old power of changing colour had been restored.

"Imagine the tree doing that in just a few minutes!" exclaimed Toby. "It must be really powerful."

"Well, it's a great relief to be hardly visible again," said the chameleon. "Thank you, O great and mighty Prism Tree. I will compose an epic poem in your honour -- when I get time."

"It seems incredible that it should need to be renewed," said Toby, "but we have to plant a cutting tonight, and it looks as if it will not be an easy task."

The tree trunk was a good ten feet round at the base, and as smooth as glass. There was not even the smallest hand- or foot-hold between the ground and the lowest branches, far out of reach. There was no way that Toby could climb it unaided, and even Hardly Visible, who could usually scuttle up a smooth wall without much trouble, took one look at it and admitted defeat.

"There must be a way," said Toby. "Can't you

think of anything? You are usually full of bright ideas."

Hardly Visible was sitting among the campions, enjoying the sensation of being red again. "I think I'll just stay here for ever," he said dreamily. "This is the chameleons' heaven. There's no place like home . . ."

"We have to save the tree, you twit!" said Toby, "or there will be no home for any of us." Then he had a bright idea himself. "I know! There are so many different kinds of trees on the slopes, some of them must have creepers growing over them, like the ones Tarzan has in the jungle. If we can find a nice, long creeper, perhaps I can manage to lasso one of the lower branches, and climb up that way. Anyway, it's our only chance. Are you coming?" Reluctantly, the chameleon tore himself away, and followed.

There were indeed creepers growing among some of the more exotic trees in the woods, but it took a couple of hours for Toby to find them, and longer still to drag one back to the clearing. They arrived back at the Prism Tree just as the sun was setting.

Toby found a smallish stone and tied it to one end of the creeper. Then he went back twenty or thirty yards from the tree, took a run, and threw the stone as if he were bowling a cricket ball. The trick worked. The stone flew over the lowest branch of the tree, and fell back to earth, pulling the creeper after it, so that it now hung down on both sides of the branch. The leaves tinkled loudly, but not one fell to the ground as the stone touched them.

"Success!" shouted Toby. Hardly Visible gave a loud squeak, but there was something about it that made Toby look round sharply.

"What's the matter?" he asked. Then he saw for himself. Emerging from the edge of the woods into the clearing was Slubblejum, waving his cutlass, and followed by a crowd of nethercats, all armed with ropes, saws and axes.

Chapter 18 ~ The End

Toby froze to the spot with horror as the nethercats came bounding towards him. He saw that Fattascratch and Bogglewick had somehow joined up with the rest of them. He grabbed the Flee Powder from where he had put it down beside the tree, and held it up so that all the nethercats could see it.

"Don't come any closer!" he shouted. "We are here to defend the Prism Tree, and I'll use the Flee Powder to send you to Timbuctoo if you try to touch it." To his astonishment, all the nethercats fell about laughing at this threat.

"He'll send us to Timbuctoo!" cackled Slubblejum.

"Or even Timbucthree!" added some wit, which set the rest of them off again. When they had calmed down a bit, Slubblejum stepped forward from the rest and announced,

"We have news for you. That Flee Powder sends people wherever they most want to go. It was that clever little pig who told us that. The old Toothsayer doesn't even know herself how it works, but the pig has nothing to do but listen to travellers' tales, and he put two and two together. Empty vessels have big ears, you know. When we heard about it, we followed you and *persuaded* you to throw it over us, without you realizing that you could have used it on yourselves."

"So we got here the easy way," grinned the tattered-looking carpenter.

"We have been bathing in a mountain stream," went on Slubblejum. "Delightful! We saw your coat and knew you had arrived, but we thought we would let you have some fun trying to climb the tree before we announced ourselves."

"Fun!" said Toby.

"Tie him up, Scratchy – we're wasting time," said Slubberjum.

"If you cut down the tree everything will mmmmmm . . ." said Toby. He had been caught by Fattascratch, who was annoyed that Slubblejum was once more in charge, and took it out on Toby, who was much smaller.

"Noisy little brat!" he said, tying a dirty old rag round Toby's mouth. "Should 'ave been gagged long since, if yer hask me!" A few minutes later,

Toby was lying on the ground near the edge of the clearing, bound hand and foot. There was no sign of Hardly Visible.

The next few hours were the worst of Toby's life. Once the sun had set, darkness had fallen much more quickly than it did at home, but to his surprise the night never became completely dark. There were hardly any clouds about, and he had forgotten how bright the stars could be. On this still, moonless night, the Milky Way could be seen clearly in a great arch across the sky. Its glimmer enabled him to see what was going on, while the nethercats, with their cat-like eyes, must have been able to see almost as well as in the daytime.

By starlight, the Prism Tree had a special, almost ghostly beauty, but the nethercats did not seem to notice it. They tied ropes round the tree, pegged them into the ground, and then attacked the trunk from both sides at once.

Almost the only sounds were those of chopping and sawing, with occasional shouts as Slubblejum or Fattascratch gave their orders – sometimes contradicting each other. A couple of times Toby heard owls hooting, and once he caught sight of a pair of night birds of some kind flying over the clearing, but apart from that everything in nature was still. That only made the raucous sounds from the nethercats seem even worse.

At last – whether it was one hour or three hours later he couldn't tell – he heard Slubblejum's voice yelling, "Tim-be-e-e-er!" There was a great, tearing, splintering sound as the mighty Prism Tree came crashing down to the ground and lay still forever.

"We're off!' shouted Slubblejum. "Nethercats rule the world!" He came bounding over to Toby.

"Where's that Flee Powder?" he demanded, pulling off the gag.

"Don't know,' muttered Toby, "And I don't care." But just then Finkleweed found the container lying on the ground.

"Good for you, Weedy!" said Slubblejum. "Let's hope there is enough left. Now, lads, all stand together and think hard of our good ship the *Catty Sark*. I'm looking forward to seeing her again." In spite of his misery, Toby almost smiled as he thought of his reaction when he found the great hole in her side. "He who laughs last lives to fight another day, and tomorrow will be the first

really grey day in history. Should just suit you, Weedy my lad!"

Then there was a mightly Whoosh! as Slubble-jum sprayed the rest of the Flee Powder over the other nethercats, then turned it on himself. He vanished, the spray gun vanishing with him, and the glade was filled with a great and terrible silence.

Toby just wanted to cry himself to sleep and never wake up again. A small squeak beside him said, "Sorry – I tried to help, but there was nothing I could do."

"Never mind, Hardly," said Toby. "There was nothing anyone could do in the end, was there?"

"I managed to bite a few of the nethercats, but it only annoyed them and made them work even faster, I'm afraid."

The rest of the night seemed to last for ever. Hardly Visible pulled the penknife out of Toby's pocket, and put it into his fingers. Toby then managed to open it, and stick the handle into the ground, so that he could rub the ropes round his wrists against the blade. As they finally gave way, he noticed vaguely that the birds were beginning their morning chorus as if nothing had happened. He untied his feet, but there was nothing to get up for. He just lay down with his face on his arms in the grass, not daring to watch the dawning of that dreadful day.

Chapter 19 ~ The Beginning

Toby lay there for what seemed a long time, hearing the bird songs without really listening to them, and putting off the moment when he would be forced to look at a grey and dying world. Hardly Visible must have reacted in the same way, but at last the warm feel of the sun made him look up, and he gave a loud squeak, "I say!"

"Leave me alone," said Toby. "I wanna die."

"But look at that!" insisted the chameleon.

'There once was a beautiful sun
That rose when the day had begun . . ."

Toby thought it was the last straw that the chameleon should start one of his silly poems at such a moment, and he raised his head to tell him to shut up. When he did so, he couldn't believe his eyes. The sun was just rising over the snowy tops of the mountains, and what a sunrise it was! The mountain tops were tinged with pink and orange; the sun was turning the clouds into a glorious skyscape of red and gold in the east, while over in the west the colours faded into green and the deepest of deep blues. He had never seen anything like it.

He stood up slowly, rubbing his eyes. The great Prism Tree was a dull grey heap on the ground. But even as he watched, the sun rose high enough above the mountains for its first rays to fall directly onto the tree. As they did so, the tree began to scorch and shrivel, as if in an invisible fire. Within a few minutes it was completely gone – vanished as if it had never existed. All that remained on the ground were a couple of axes and ropes abandoned by the nethercats, and the rings of bright flowers. In the middle there was now only a space of clear green grass where the stump of the tree had been.

Toby felt completely stunned. He wondered if all he had been told about the Prism Tree had been wrong after all. But then he remembered the effect it had had on the chameleon, and turned to look for his little friend. At that moment, he noticed a pair of birds flying over the tree tops in a very purposeful way. As they drew near, he recognized Dee Lee, with a colourful Mandarin drake at her side.

The duck and drake landed beside him in such a flurry of excitement that for a few minutes he could hardly make out what they were talking about. But after he had been well and truly introduced to Dah Lee, and Dee Lee had said at least fifty times how glad she was to see him, they at last sat down on the grass, with Hardly Visible perched on Toby's shoulder, and the ducks began their story.

Dee Lee seemed determined to make up in words what she lacked in colour beside her handsome husband, and she did most of the talking.

"It was all thanks to the Toothsayer," she began. "As soon as you left her she started thinking how to save us. Then she found your watch outside her house – the strap must have slipped. So she decided to use it to make the Emperor a clockwork nightingale. It did not take her long, as she is so clever at inventing things, and she at once took it to the palace, leaving that pig of hers to mind the house."

"That must have been when Slubblejum and his pals arrived," said Toby.

"I don't know about that, but anyway, the Toothsayer knew from your story not to say anything about exchange. She simply offered the clockwork nightingale as a free and generous gift, and insisted that it should be given to the Emperor at once, because it would help to cure his cold. And do you know, she was quite right. His cold was cured within the hour."

"He was probably better anyway," put in Dah Lee. "The old fraud just stayed in bed because he was too bored to do anything else."

"*I'm* telling this story," said his wife. "You make everything sound so *ordinary*. Well, the main thing is that the Emperor was so fascinated by the clockwork nightingale that he lost interest in ducks. Also, he wanted the cage to make the nightingale look more realistic. So he turned us out of the cage where we had been squashed in together . . ."

"Much better than being in there on my own!" said Dah Lee.

". . . and let us fly out of the window. Well, the Toothsayer was waiting for us outside, and she told us to fly after you. She had a feeling in her bones that you might be in need of help. But it was so difficult to fly over the mountains. Yesterday morning I just couldn't fly another flap. If it hadn't been for that yeti . . ."

"Yeti!" exclaimed Toby and Hardly Visible together.

"Yes, he gave us a lift the rest of the way, and dropped us at the edge of the valley just before nightfall. When we reached the glade, the nethercats were just starting their dirty work. Dah Lee managed to break off a small twig with his beak while the nethercats were busy with their ropes — they never thought of looking up.

"But we knew that the twig must be planted among the violets, and of course all the violets in the glade were overrun by nethercats. So we had to fly off and search through the trees in the dark to find another patch of violets. It seemed to take hours, and even then we couldn't be sure it had worked. But it has, it has!" she concluded, flapping up and down in excitement. "You must come and see it."

Toby and Hardly Visible followed the ducks as they half flew, half waddled through the trees until they came to a very small glade, only a few yards across. Here they all stopped in astonishment. The little Prism Tree, its tiny leaves glinting in the sunlight, was standing firmly upright in the middle of a clump of violets, as they had expected. But they had not expected that it would already be nearly three feet high, and visibly growing before their eyes. As they stood and watched, they could see the little branches stretching out inch by inch, and new little buds opening out into glittering leaves, like living diamonds.

It was clear that before the day was out the new Prism Tree would already be taller than the other trees around it. Indeed, the trees nearest it seemed to be dwindling as it grew bigger, as if their life and energy were somehow being absorbed into the greater life of the Prism Tree. As the new prism leaves opened out, they were at once beginning the chiming, tinkling music of the old tree.

It was a long time before anyone spoke. Then it was Hardly Visible who broke the silence, which he did by saying, "Does anyone think it's time for breakfast?"

So the boy, the chameleon and the pair of ducks sat down together beside the new Prism Tree, and had a picnic of fruit, or squiggly things, or both, according to taste.

"Strange how we all like different things," remarked Hardly Visible. "My favourite are stick insects – when I can get them. And yetis like sweets . . . among other things.

"Oh, the yeti isn't pretty
And the yeti isn't smart,
But I really must admit he
Has a very tender heart;

For he loves the little birdies
That he sees upon his way,
And he waves to bunny rabbits
As they innocently play.

He has mountaineers for dinner,
Often starting with their feet,
But we really mustn't blame him –
Even yetis have to eat!"

"You made it up!" said Toby. "Plonk was very nice to us, anyway. But we have no yeti to give us a lift now – how are we all going to get home again?"

"We'll just fly back to China in easy stages, the way we came," said Dah Lee.

"Though we will still have problems when we get there," added his wife. "Pond-hunting can be very difficult for newly-weds, you know."

"Never mind, dear, we'll manage," said Dah Lee.

"Let's just stay here forever," said Hardly Visible –

"That's all very well for chameleons," said Toby, as he bit into his *very* last apple, "but I think I would get tired of eating fruit and doing nothing after a day or two. I'll just have to hitch-hike all the way back to England, I suppose. What a nuisance!"

"Why not go by Flee Powder Express?" said the Toothsayer. Toby choked on his piece of apple, and had to be slapped on the back by the cackling Toothsayer, while the ducks flew squawking up into the air until they recovered from their fright.

"How . . . How did you get here?" Toby managed to splutter at last.

"How do you think?" said the Toothsayer. "I was finally put wise about the Flee Powder by a returning traveller. Imagine inventing something, and not realizing how it works yourself! Well, it has happened before, and no doubt it will happen again. My, my – just look at that!" she added.

*"I think that I shall never see
A poem like the Prism Tree!"*

She went over to admire the rapidly growing tree. "Well, at least this one is safe for another few million years," she said. "But the balance of nature depends on all the ordinary trees – if only people would stop cutting *them* down. Dracula's dentures! Why don't they just stop to think before they destroy things. And it won't be much use us saving the Prism Tree if they blot out the sunlight with smoke and fumes and such-like." She heaved a big sigh.

"I never saw so many kinds of trees," said Toby. "I think I'll be a tree-ologist when I grow up. Is that the right word?"

"What's in a word?" said the Toothsayer. "Be a sunshine-ologist if you like. Now, where's that Flee Powder?" She pulled the new spray gun from her pocket.

"It's strange that Shep never told you how the Flee Powder works," said Toby.

"Vipers' biters!" said the Toothsayer. "If I ever lay eyes on that Small Hairy Earth Pig again, I'll make his teeth rattle! But I don't suppose I will. He was never really tame, you know, and he seems to have run off back to the wild. I'll get something docile for a pet next time, like a . . ."

"Like a pair of ducks?" suggested Dee Lee shyly. "I did so admire that lotus pool of yours, and we are looking for a home, you know."

"Dee, my dear!" exclaimed Dah Lee. "That is rather a cheek, you know."

"Not at all!" said the Toothsayer. "You would be very welcome, and an ornament to the pond, if I may say so. It's an excellent idea – wish I had thought of it myself. By the way, how did you like my idea about the clockwork nightingale?"

"Great!" said Toby.

"It is not strictly clockwork, of course," went on the Toothsayer, "but it is certainly original. It must be the only quartz digital nightingale in the world that sings *Jingle Bells*. Now, we had better all stand together, and think of where we want to go. Ready? Where's Hardly Visible?"

"I want to stay here," said a small squeak. "Or do I? I think perhaps . . ."

But what he thought Toby never knew, because the Flee Powder had already been squeezed over them all.

Epilogue

Toby woke with a bump in the little rowing boat near the shore of the lake. At least, it *felt* like waking up, but he knew it was really the effect of the Flee Powder. One of his oars was floating in the water a few yards away, but he managed to lean over and rescue it.

"Hi, Grandma!" he said, as he landed the boat. "You'll never guess – I've just been helping to save the world from extinction."

Grandma was busy painting. "Oh yes, dear," she said. "That's nice."

Then Toby told her all about his adventures. She said, "Fancy that!" when he told her about flying on the back of a dragon, and "I've always wanted to meet one of those things," when he got to the bit about the yeti. As he finished his story, she said, "Oh, I am stiff!" and started putting her paints away.

"Don't say you've lost your watch!" she added.

Toby looked at his empty wrist, and said, "But I told you . . ."

"Yes, you did tell me it needed a new strap," she said. "Well, if you're good I'll get you another one – but not till the day you are going home, mind! That was a good story about your travels," she went on. "I've always wanted to travel myself, but somehow I never get round to it.

"I'd love to go a-wandering
To places far and wide,
But now I think it looks like rain –
Perhaps I'll stay inside.

I'd love to take a sailing ship
Across the seas to roam,
But I get seasick every time –
Perhaps I'll stay at home.

I'd love to climb intrepidly
A rocky mountain peak,
But mountains can be rather cold –
Perhaps I'll go next week."

Today I'd rather stay right here
And switch on the TV –
I'll watch the great explorers
While I have my toast and tea.

"Run along and put the kettle on, would you, Toby?"